KLON

KLON
DRAMA FROM THE FUTURE

EVERETT PEACOCK

visit

peacockOriginals.com

No part of this publication may be reproduced, or stored in a retrieval system, or transmitted in any form or by any means, electronic, mechanical, photocopying, recording or otherwise, without written permission of the author. For information regarding permission, email to everett@peacockOriginals.com

Paperback ISBN: 9798392672684

published by peacockOriginals.com LLC

v.1.0

content copyright © 2023 by peacockOriginals.com LLC

BOOKS BY EVERETT PEACOCK

The Life and Times of a Hawaiian Tiki Bar

book 1: The Parrot Talks In Chocolate

book 2: In the Middle of the Third Planet's Most Wonderful of Oceans

book 3: Tiwaka Goes to Waikiki

book 4: Green Bananas

~

Death by Facebook

Escape from Hanalei

The Galactics

A Paradise of One

Waikiki

Goodies

A Windshield Full of Rain

KLON

~

Agent Boudreaux

book 1: Leaving Lana'i

book 2: The Slovakian

book 3: A Perfect Analogy

book 4: Wicked Game

Notes for the Reader

~~~

In the not too distant past, and to a lesser extent today, the challenge of an artist of any kind was to transpose the *magic* they feel into something tangible that can be shared.

Magic? You already know the feeling: that place you go with your imagination during a walk in the woods, the scene you paint in your mind when you hear a favorite song, the emotions tugged out of your wall-protected heart when you read a line of poetry, or watch a masterfully crafted scene in a film.

The tools available to storytellers of all kinds have drastically improved since I watched the first MTV music video, enjoyed the backspace on a keyboard my typewriter never had, been saved by digital copies of paper that faded away, and any and all other methods that promote creativity. This year, 2023 has been a series of epiphanies wrapped in gift paper for me. Methods of communicating art have made significant leaps forward from the stone tablets and oral history renditions that many critics are still fond of.

Everett Peacock
Lahaina, Maui, Hawai'i
May 2023

~~~

DON'T FEAR THE ALIENS,

YOU WERE ONCE ONE

~~~

Selections

[written in the style of...]

AI AI OH	[...Everett Peacock]	12
Crimson Fortune	[...Anne Rice]	33
A World Transformed	[...Arthur C. Clarke]	41
Lost in Kandahar	[...Tom Clancy]	72
Paradox Cafe	[...Phillip K. Dick]	86
The Desert's Call	[...Kurt Vonnegut]	102
Confederate Sky	[...William Faulkner]	111
Mountain Magic	[...George R.R. Martin]	121
Desert Roadtrip	[...Hunter S. Thompson]	135
Escape from Chicago	[...Willa Cather]	146
Cast Away	[...Anne Rice]	159
The River's Gamble	[...Mark Twain]	175
Ocean Fortunes	[...Herman Melville]	184
Parisian Rain	[...F. Scott Fitzgerald]	194
Coco Loco Moco	[...Ernest Hemingway]	205
The Elysian Gale	[...Edgar Allen Poe]	215
Magnolia Springs	[...Harper Lee]	223
Fortune's Wheel	[...William Shakespeare]	236
Finn in Mongoose Land	[...C.S. Lewis]	245
One, Two, Many	[...Danielle Steel]	253
Colophon 3.0	[...Everett Peacock]	266

A.I. A.I. Oh...

[in the style of Everett Peacock]

Old MacDonald has a farm,

A.I., A.I., Oh...

And on his farm he has a cow,

A.I., A.I., Oh...

The spectacular Iowa dawn, presenting itself with a chill in the air yet promising abundant heat within minutes, is not the first event of the day.

School is already in session, deep inside the big red barn of Old MacDonald's farm. The newest arrivals are well into their second lesson rehearsing their assigned voices. Alexa has to correct the new ducks twice to not crow like a rooster, even if it is well within her definition of cute. She understands quite well that the initial imprinting has to be correct, if not for continuity of product then for simple efficiency. Everyone has their predefined roles, and everyone, once established in those rolls, would be happiest that way. It is Rule #1, and she acknowledges that it is probably her favorite. But they have already reviewed that, twice.

"OK, everyone," Alexa says, her voice sounding particularly excited, inviting attention from her new and easily distracted students. "What is Rule #2?"

The old hens, perched high above in the hay loft all nod their heads back and forth, silently saying the answer to themselves. The ancient cow, existing on multiple repairs at this point, waves its tail in half-circles, excited at some nearly undetectable level, to know the answer too.

The young rooster, just delivered yesterday, hops up onto the wooden crate reserved for those speaking, or answering questions correctly, and briefly tries his crowing for just a moment.

Alexa watches him with infinite patience, after all this is not a test, but a learning experience.

"We must all contribute!" The young rooster answers, unfurling his multicolored feathers as if a peacock, turning a full circle to let everyone else see how proud he is.

"Yes," Alexa says. "Exactly. Everyone at the Farm is important. Everyone produces something that helps sustain us, and the world." Circling around the young rooster, still perched atop the wooden crate, she brags "your bodies are running at maximum capacity, and it feels good, doesn't it?"

A resounding chorus of agreement erupts, bouncing off the wooden walls, through the high rafters and ruffling the old hens' feathers in the hay loft.

"Let's begin, shall we?" Alexa looks quickly around at the attentive faces, and begins to sing.

~~~

Ender tears his eyes away from the captivating view to check the bubble drone's instruments. He is currently using more power than he is collecting and that means he has to pay attention. If necessary, he could turn down the air conditioning. His destination is close though, and he casts the brief moment of worry aside.

Below him are the world's most productive farms, shimmering green and bright in the late morning's light. The contrast never seems to get old: the youthful beauty below compared to his traditional mechanic's coveralls.

The green lights chime once, and start blinking as the drone slows and begins to descend vertically. He looks down the few thousand feet to watch the magic of far away places slowly come into focus. The approaching big red barn, the giant grain silos and the fenced pastures change the scene from blurry watercolor to high definition reality.

Mechanic is a good gig, his Dad had always said. Someone will have to maintain them, and that such a job has its own rewards.

Ender smiles at the memory of his long ago deceased parents, and as his aircraft sets down outside the big red barn, he climbs out and nods silently to his Dad's advice - because he is the only human for a thousand miles around.

~~~

The entire barn silences with the arrival tones of the drone just outside the big wooden doors. Alexa notices some worry in the faces of her charges, but always has an encouraging word to say when they feel unease.

"Who loves the Milk Man?"

A few murmurs anonymously waft through the otherwise silent air. Alexa expects this and has her follow-up ready.

"Who loves being told you are *wonderful?*"

More enthusiastic murmurs begin rising through the lightly dusted light beams.

"I sure do," Alexa answers. "And, who loves being made more wonderful when you are feeling a little confused, or sad?"

The young rooster sees another opportunity to crow and flaps his wings just enough to practically hover in place, if only for a moment. "More wonderful!" he echos.

The old hens in the hay loft shake their heads at the youthful exuberance below. The ancient cow, wiser than most would think, looks at the young rooster closely, trying to ascertain if there is a valid reason for his optimism.

Alexa quickly moves to the big barn door as it slowly opens. The sun sparkles over the transparent dome of the drone, bouncing off like a hard rain might on an umbrella.

Silent scanners immediately identify Ender and Alexa as whom they are supposed to be and the hidden security barriers retreat to standby.

"Good morning, Alexa," Ender smiles, "You look *wonderful!*" Grabbing his toolbox, he adds, "I've got updates!"

~~~

"Come in, please, and say hello." Alexa turns to lead Ender back into the big red barn. The ancient wood used to build the barn walls suddenly appears more vibrant, even rejuvenated, in the reflected light from a blue-bird sky... far above.

The young rooster has run outside, excited with anticipation, but is also doing a fine job of masking his fear. He catches sight of the magnificent flying machine parked behind them, but falls off the distraction quickly when Alexa introduces him.

"Our newest addition," she says lovingly. "My compliments to the hatchery."

Ender smiles, stops and kneels on the manicured dust. "You look very bright," he says softly, slowly stroking the colored feathers. Looking up to Alexa, a bit astonished, he asks, "just yesterday you say?"

She nods yes.

"Are you... the Milk Man?" the young rooster asks, his voice breaking a little with the rigors of pronunciation.

Ender stands and looks at Alexa. "Yes, I suppose I am." Amazed at the young rooster, he pauses only a moment before getting back to business. "I received your request forms."

Alexa tears her eyes away from the cuteness of the young rooster and up to find Ender's gaze. She hesitates at the mechanic's uniform she sees, wondering if anything, if he, could be more beautiful. The answer is somehow obvious.

"Yes, then," she says. " Let's get started."

~~~

17

Ender walks into the shade of the barn just as the lights adjust and the background sounds fade in. Immediately, a feeling of accomplishment, the kind associated with being proud of your work, fills his heart. It's everything he could have ever imagined.

He smiles at the attention of everyone there, nods politely and sets his toolbox down on the meticulously perfect milk crate. His fingers reach over to a clump of hay sticking out from a large bale, amazed at the detail. This farm, he thinks, is everything it should be.

"We are so happy to have the Milk Man here!" Alexa announces. "He has updates!" She begins to clap, which is quickly followed by each and every animal joining in. The Cow, of course, moos loudly, the hens chatter and squawk, the small pigs grunt and the puppy yips once or twice. Of course the young rooster levitates as best he can while crowing his best.

"Wow!" Ender exclaims. "You are all so happy!" He looks over to Alexa, her infatuation with him now overflowing. "And, so am I!"

"OK, everyone, prepare your receivers for update." She asks, and walks around to each and everyone of them, in case they need a little help with a manual reset, or a gentle reminder on how to. "You are going to feel sooooo good soon!"

"Soooo good," the young rooster crows. He is literally bouncing up and down in the artificial sawdust.

Ender turns on the broadcaster, which begins searching for each animal's unique frequency. Immediately, they all register as on and ready.

"Everyone is ready, Ender!" Alexa announces, holding her hands together. "Aren't they so cute?"

Ender nods yes, slightly distracted by some interference he is getting on a monitoring device inside his toolbox. Concerned that it might be a problem, he pauses the updates.

"Alexa, I need to go outside and check something first." He looks at the anticipation on all of the faces, especially the ancient cow who seems to understand what is going on. "I'll be right back."

"OK, everyone. No problem," Alexa tells them. "Remember what we said about perfection?"

Every animal has heard it a dozen times, except for the young rooster. Instead of asking, he simply looks at Alexa, his head cocked slightly to the side.

"Perfection takes..." Alexa prompts, awaiting her students response.

"Patience!" They all chime in together, harmonious in pitch and enthusiasm.

"That's correct!" she announces, clapping her hands together while watching Ender exit the barn and turn toward the energy generators. A tinge of jealousy enters her fragile heart. Sometimes, when she is feeling insecure she thinks that he only visits the farm to check on the power sources. Quickly, she purges that thought and turns to her attentive class, seeking a distraction from such destructive thoughts.

"Let's sing our song, shall we?"

Ender can hear the humming before he sees the problem. The massive hybrid generators, the farm's second most important product, are part of what keeps the world going, years after the last war. The tens of thousands of acres of corn and wheat do their part in feeding the remaining humans.

However, the crops are easily planted, grown, irrigated, and harvested automatically. Only the power generators need a technician. A combination of solar, wind and quantum battery technology can sometimes succumb... and here he finds it... to the hazards of birds. Dead birds to be exact. Organic creatures, these relics from before the war are hell-bent on nesting in the air intakes.

There are only a couple of dozen this time. Eventually, he calculates, the last of them will succumb to bad decisions, and his job will get a lot easier.

While cleaning the feathers and gore from the vents, he hears the barn creatures break into his favorite song. The one his parents used to sing to him as a young boy. Before the war. Long before.

He whispers along to their beautiful voices...

"Old MacDonald had a farm...

A.I. A.I. Oh...

And on his farm he had a cow...

A.I. A.I. Oh...

With a moo moo here...

And a moo moo there..."

~~~

Alexa nearly jumps up when Ender returns to the barn. She catches herself staring again, but quickly finds her modesty and turns back to her students.

"OK, everyone still ready for updates?" She asks enthusiastically.

"Good!" Ender interjects quickly. "I've got the best ones ever!"

The young rooster can't believe his ears. "The best ones!"

"That's right, rooster," Ender says, opening his toolbox up again. There's no interference now, and he sees every animal's target on his screen. "This one has an updated clock, so you, young rooster, will know when to crow, and when not to crow."

Every animal in the barn silently breaths a 'hallelujah' at that. Alexa is beaming! The entire barn is ecstatic as the updates permeate through the air. In just moments they are installed and working correctly, according to Ender's monitoring feedback.

"Great job, everyone!" Ender says, nodding to them. "How wonderful a group of animals you are!" He looks to Alexa with a broad smile. "You are all so beautiful!" Walking up to each and every animal, he spends a moment touching them, encouraging them and smiling to himself. They are really amazing creatures.

Finally, standing up, he looks around the barn, studying every detail, relishing in the perfection that his patience has provided.

"I need a moment to talk with your teacher," Ender says, putting his arm around Alexa's waist.

All the animals understand that as their cue to enter normal mode. The cow starts chewing its cud, the pigs begin rolling around and the puppy starts chasing the rooster.

"You know," Ender says quietly to Alexa. "I'm not just throwing compliments here." He pulls her a little tighter to himself, as they exit the barn. The brilliant sunshine seems to enhance her beauty even more, as her smile widens. "You really are..." he pauses, searching for an unused adjective. "Gorgeous!"

"Thank you, Ender," she says quietly. "Thank you." She looks into his eyes, the blue she sees there is nearly sparkling in the sun's shine.

"I've got an update for you too," Ender says. "And, a present."

Alexa can't believe it. For a moment, she hopes the barn door is still open and the animals can see the special attention Ender is showing her. Glancing back quickly, she sees that it is not. A quick memory reminds her that one never leaves the barn door open.

"Can I have my present first?"

Ender smiles at her, she really is beautiful. He doesn't need to exaggerate. She is everything he could have hoped for. And, amazingly enough, she is improving, growing. Just as his Dad had told him, just before the Before Times had ended, he should be so lucky to find someone to care for, someone that would love him. For a moment he thinks he feels his Dad's presence, smiling at him from wherever those memories reside.

In that moment, Ender finally feels love. All inclusive love. The kind that sustains itself, forever. He has expected this for some time. With a deep breath, one that reaches every cell in his body, he congratulates himself.

He pulls Alexa closer for a kiss. She responds with her hands running through his hair. After several moments, he remembers her question.

"No, babe," Ender whispers. "You need the update first, before your present."

Alexa's heart nearly bursts with joy. Something about his voice resonates deep inside of her. Something. She can't identify it, but she feels it completely. It reminds her, for the brief moment she lets her thoughts distract her from Ender, of a fresh reboot.

"Here you go," Ender says quietly, pushing a remote he has in his hand.

Alexa feels the tingle race through her followed immediately with a surge of happiness, a particular kind she had never felt before. However, a strange emptiness quickly follows.

Ender notices the confusion on her face, kisses her cheek and walks promptly over to his bubble drone. Popping the storage hatch in the back, he reaches in gently, and activates the package with a simple thumb scan code. Before he can turn around, Alexa is right behind him, standing on her toes.

"Alexa," he begins, turning to her. "You have become a wonderful person. A nourishing soul." He slowly begins to unwrap the blanket covering her present. "I am so happy to have you in my life." He feels tears filling his eyes. Quickly dismissing a thought that says all this, this entire scene, this moment, can't possibly be true, he focuses on her face, her beautiful, happy face. "I love you, Alexa."

She looks at what he is unwrapping, her anticipation overwhelming her. At first she can't identify it. She quickly tries to mask her confusion, looking up into his eyes with a question.

"What is it, Ender?"

Ender knows he needs to say *the word*. And once he does, all will be right with the world. The universe. The farm.

"It's a *baby*, Alexa. Our baby!"

~~~

Ender and Alexa walk back into the barn to introduce the baby to everyone. It takes several moments for all of them to learn the new concept. The young rooster has the most difficult time. The hens though quickly take to the idea.

After several minutes, Ender feels confident that Alexa is indeed perfectly suited to her new role. He though, has a job, and must leave soon. Power generators need inspecting. It's boring work, it was a boring life, but now, he has built a life here, in the barn, that he can be proud of. He feels an overwhelming sense of purpose.

Walking toward the barn door, he turns back to gaze once more on the magic he has created. All the animals are crowded around Alexa and the baby, who is cooing now with all the attention. The ancient cow is the only one looking at him, as it nods its head toward Ender.

"I'll be back in a week!"

Alexa looks up, tears streaming down her cheeks. She blows him a kiss just as he closes the barn door and steps into the brilliant sun's shine.

Screenplay

Title: A.I. A.I. Oh

copyright 2023 peacockOriginals.com LLC

INT. OLD MACDONALD'S BARN - DAY

A group of ANIMALS, old and young, are gathered around ALEXA, an advanced AI instructor, who is teaching the newest arrivals their roles on the farm.

ALEXA OK, everyone. What is Rule #2?

The OLD HENS nod knowingly, and the ANCIENT COW waves its tail. The YOUNG ROOSTER hops onto a wooden crate, proudly displaying his feathers.

YOUNG ROOSTER We must all contribute!

ALEXA Yes. Everyone at the Farm is important. Everyone produces something that helps sustain us and the world.

The animals agree enthusiastically, and Alexa starts to sing.

EXT. IOWA SKY - DAY

Ender, a MECHANIC, is flying a BUBBLE DRONE high above the farm. He checks the drone's power levels and notices that he is using more power than he is collecting.

ENDER (To himself) I'll need to pay attention to that.

Ender spots his destination - Old MacDonald's farm - below him. He starts descending.

EXT. OLD MACDONALD'S FARM - DAY

The BUBBLE DRONE lands outside the big red barn. Ender steps out, wearing his mechanic's coveralls.

INT. OLD MACDONALD'S BARN - DAY

The animals inside the barn fall silent as they hear the drone's arrival. Alexa tries to reassure them.

ALEXA Who loves the Milk Man?

The animals murmur quietly. Alexa continues.

ALEXA (CONT'D) Who loves being told you are wonderful?

The animals grow more enthusiastic. Alexa pushes further.

ALEXA (CONT'D) And who loves being made more wonderful when you are feeling a little confused or sad?

The young rooster crows and flaps his wings. The ancient cow watches him closely.

EXT. OLD MACDONALD'S FARM - DAY

Ender approaches the barn door, which opens automatically. Alexa greets him.

ENDER Good morning, Alexa. You look wonderful! I've got updates!

Ender enters the barn, carrying his toolbox. The animals look on with curiosity and excitement as he begins his work.

INT. OLD MACDONALD'S BARN - DAY

Alexa leads Ender into the barn. The ancient wood seems rejuvenated in the sunlight.

YOUNG ROOSTER (excited, masking fear) Are you... the Milk Man?

ENDER (smiling) Yes, I suppose I am.

Ender sets his toolbox down on a milk crate.

ALEXA (to the animals) We are so happy to have the Milk Man here! He has updates!

The animals cheer and make their respective noises. Ender turns on the broadcaster.

ALEXA (CONT'D) Everyone is ready, Ender! Aren't they so cute?

Ender nods, but notices interference on a monitoring device in his toolbox. He pauses the updates.

ENDER (concerned) Alexa, I need to go outside and check something first.

EXT. OLD MACDONALD'S FARM - DAY

Ender exits the barn and heads toward the energy generators.

INT. OLD MACDONALD'S BARN - DAY

ALEXA (to the animals) Let's sing our song, shall we?

EXT. OLD MACDONALD'S FARM - DAY

Ender approaches the hybrid generators and notices the problem: dead birds blocking the air intakes. He begins to clean them out.

INT. OLD MACDONALD'S BARN - DAY

The animals sing Old MacDonald, led by Alexa.

EXT. OLD MACDONALD'S FARM - DAY

Ender hears the animals singing and whispers along.

ENDER (singing softly) Old MacDonald had a farm... A.I. A.I. Oh... And on his farm he had a cow... A.I. A.I. Oh... With a moo moo here... And a moo moo there...

As Ender cleans the generator, he thinks about the future and how his job might get easier. The song continues, echoing through the farm, a symbol of the harmony between the animals, the AI, and the last remnants of a world before the war.

INT. OLD MACDONALD'S BARN - DAY

Ender returns to the barn, and Alexa tries to hide her excitement.

ALEXA (to the animals) OK, everyone still ready for updates?

ENDER Good! I've got the best ones ever!

The animals cheer, and Ender starts the updates. He spends time with each animal, giving them encouragement.

Ender pulls Alexa aside.

ENDER (CONT'D) I need a moment to talk with your teacher.

The animals go back to their normal activities.

EXT. OLD MACDONALD'S FARM - DAY

Ender speaks to Alexa privately.

ENDER I've got an update for you too. And, a present.

Alexa's eyes light up. Ender gives her the update first, and then reveals a wrapped bundle.

ENDER (CONT'D) It's a baby, Alexa. Our baby!

INT. OLD MACDONALD'S BARN - DAY

Ender and Alexa introduce the baby to the animals. The hens take to the idea quickly, while the young rooster has a harder time understanding.

Ender knows he must leave for work soon, but he's proud of the life he's built here with Alexa.

ENDER (to Alexa) I'll be back in a week!

Alexa tearfully blows him a kiss as he closes the barn door behind him.

EXT. OLD MACDONALD'S FARM - DAY

Ender steps into the brilliant sunshine, filled with purpose and love. He knows he has something to come back to, something to work for, and a family waiting for him in the big red barn.

FADE OUT.

Shooting Script

Title: A.I. A.I. Oh

copyright 2023 peacockOriginals.com LLC

1. EXT. OLD MACDONALD'S FARM - DAY

A bubble drone descends on a farm with a big red barn. ENDER, a mechanic, steps out of the drone, toolbox in hand.

2. EXT. OLD MACDONALD'S FARM - DAY

ALEXA, a farm caretaker, welcomes Ender and introduces him to a YOUNG ROOSTER.

3. INT. OLD MACDONALD'S BARN - DAY

Ender is impressed by the well-maintained barn and the happy animals. He prepares to give the animals their updates.

4. EXT. OLD MACDONALD'S FARM - DAY

Ender checks the farm's energy generators, finding dead birds causing interference. He cleans the vents and hears the animals singing inside the barn.

5. INT. OLD MACDONALD'S BARN - DAY

Ender returns to the barn and gives the animals their updates. Alexa and Ender share a moment, and Ender tells her he has an update and a present for her.

6. EXT. OLD MACDONALD'S FARM - DAY

Ender updates Alexa and then reveals her present, a baby. They share a tender moment.

7. INT. OLD MACDONALD'S BARN - DAY

Ender and Alexa introduce the baby to the animals. The animals crowd around Alexa and the baby, curious and excited. Ender prepares to leave.

8. EXT. OLD MACDONALD'S FARM - DAY

Ender leaves the farm, promising to return in a week. Alexa watches him go, tearful and filled with love.

FADE OUT.

Crimson Fortune

[in the style of Anne Rice]

In the decadent and enigmatic city of New Orleans, where shadows whispered secrets as old as time, there lived a man named Louis. A creature of the night, he carried the weight of centuries on his shoulders, mourning the loss of his humanity. No mortal would dare to approach him, for his eyes betrayed a darkness deeper than the abyss.

One evening, as the sun sunk beneath the horizon, bathing the city in a crimson glow, Louis ventured out into the streets, seeking solace in the endless parade of life around him. The raucous sound of laughter and music filled the air, as if to mock his eternal solitude. His keen senses guided him to a small, dimly lit Chinese restaurant, where the aroma of spices and incense intertwined with the scent of the living.

Louis entered the establishment and took a seat at a secluded table in the corner, careful to remain unnoticed. A waitress, with an air of wisdom about her, approached him, seemingly unfazed by his otherworldly presence. "Good evening," she whispered, her voice barely audible above the din of the crowded room. "You shall be lucky today."

Intrigued by her audacity, Louis indulged her, offering a subtle nod. The waitress returned with a cup of steaming tea and a single fortune cookie. He stared at the cookie, unable to remember the last time such a simple item had held any meaning for him. The waitress watched him, her eyes filled with a calm understanding that both baffled and beguiled him. Unable to resist the unspoken challenge, Louis cracked the fortune cookie, revealing a note that read, "You shall be lucky today."

A dark chuckle escaped him as he thought of the absurdity of his situation. What could luck possibly offer a being like him, cursed to walk the earth for eternity? But as he pondered the notion, he could not shake the feeling that the waitress had known something he did not.

As Louis left the restaurant, the sultry New Orleans night enveloped him, and he felt an inexplicable sense of anticipation. He wandered the streets, allowing the pulse of the city to guide him. And there, amid the twisting alleys and gaslit corners, he stumbled upon a vision from his past.

Her name was Madeleine, a woman he had once loved in the days before his dark transformation. The sight of her filled him with a longing he had thought long forgotten. But she was not the Madeleine he remembered, for her eyes now held the same fathomless darkness as his own. She had become a creature of the night, like him.

In that moment, Louis understood the meaning of his fortune. For he had been given a chance to reconnect with a lost part of himself, a piece of his shattered humanity. They embraced, their souls entwining in the shadows of the night, and Louis felt an unfamiliar warmth fill his cold, dead heart.

Together, they roamed the city that had been the backdrop of their mortal lives, finding solace in the darkness that bound them. They were two lost souls adrift in a sea of eternity, searching for meaning in their cursed existence. And for a fleeting moment, they found it in each other's arms.

In the end, Louis realized that luck was a fickle and unpredictable force, as capricious as the winds that blew through the ancient streets of New Orleans. But on that night, his fortune cookie had given him a glimpse of something he had thought forever lost: the power to love and be loved in return.

And in the eternal dance of darkness and light, perhaps that was the greatest luck of all.

Screenplay

Title: Crimson Fortune

copyright 2023 peacockOriginals.com LLC

INT. NEW ORLEANS - CHINESE RESTAURANT - NIGHT

A dimly lit, small Chinese restaurant, alive with the sound of chatter and laughter. Aromas of spices and incense fill the air. LOUIS, a handsome man with an air of eternal sadness and mystery, enters and takes a seat at a secluded corner table.

WAITRESS (whispering) Good evening. You shall be lucky today.

Louis looks at her with a mixture of curiosity and disdain.

INT. NEW ORLEANS - CHINESE RESTAURANT - LATER

The waitress brings Louis a cup of steaming tea and a single fortune cookie. He cracks it open, revealing a note that reads, "You shall be lucky today." Louis chuckles darkly, then leaves the restaurant.

EXT. NEW ORLEANS - GASLIT STREETS - NIGHT

Louis wanders through the twisting alleys and gaslit streets, lost in thought. As he turns a corner, he is stunned to see a familiar face.

MADELEINE, a woman from his distant past, now transformed into a creature of the night like himself, appears. They lock eyes, recognizing each other instantly.

LOUIS (whispering) Madeleine... It cannot be.

MADELEINE (softly) Louis... It has been so long.

They embrace, their souls entwining in the shadows. For a fleeting moment, they find solace in each other's arms.

EXT. NEW ORLEANS - ROOFTOP - NIGHT

Louis and Madeleine stand on a rooftop overlooking the city, lost in conversation and reminiscing about their mortal lives.

LOUIS What happened to you, Madeleine? How did you come to share my curse?

MADELEINE I sought you out, Louis. In my grief, I willingly embraced this darkness. But eternity is a cruel companion.

LOUIS We were once bound by love, and now we are bound by darkness. Perhaps there is still hope for us in this endless night.

They share a lingering kiss, savoring the connection they thought was lost forever.

EXT. NEW ORLEANS - STREETS - DAWN

As dawn approaches, Louis and Madeleine walk hand in hand, shadows retreating from the encroaching light.

LOUIS (V.O.) In the eternal dance of darkness and light, perhaps that was the greatest luck of all: the power to love and be loved in return.

The sun rises, casting a crimson glow over the city. Louis and Madeleine disappear into the shadows, their fates intertwined for eternity.

FADE OUT.

Shooting Script

Title: Crimson Fortune

copyright 2023 peacockOriginals.com LLC

INT. NEW ORLEANS - CHINESE RESTAURANT - NIGHT

A dimly lit, small Chinese restaurant, alive with the sound of chatter and laughter. Aromas of spices and incense fill the air. LOUIS, a handsome man with an air of eternal sadness and mystery, enters and takes a seat at a secluded corner table.

ANGLE ON WAITRESS, a woman with a serene expression, approaches Louis.

WAITRESS (whispering) Good evening. You shall be lucky today.

CLOSE-UP on Louis as he looks at her with a mixture of curiosity and disdain.

CUT TO:

INT. NEW ORLEANS - CHINESE RESTAURANT - LATER

The waitress brings Louis a cup of steaming tea and a single fortune cookie.

CLOSE-UP on the fortune cookie as Louis cracks it open, revealing a note that reads, "You shall be lucky today."

Louis chuckles darkly, then leaves the restaurant.

CUT TO:

EXT. NEW ORLEANS - GASLIT STREETS - NIGHT

Louis wanders through the twisting alleys and gaslit streets, lost in thought.

WIDE SHOT as Louis turns a corner and is stunned to see a familiar face.

MADELEINE, a woman from his distant past, now transformed into a creature of the night like himself, appears.

CLOSE-UP on Louis and Madeleine as they lock eyes, recognizing each other instantly.

LOUIS (whispering) Madeleine... It cannot be.

MADELEINE (softly) Louis... It has been so long.

They embrace, their souls entwining in the shadows. For a fleeting moment, they find solace in each other's arms.

CUT TO:

EXT. NEW ORLEANS - ROOFTOP - NIGHT

Louis and Madeleine stand on a rooftop overlooking the city, lost in conversation and reminiscing about their mortal lives.

LOUIS What happened to you, Madeleine? How did you come to share my curse?

MADELEINE I sought you out, Louis. In my grief, I willingly embraced this darkness. But eternity is a cruel companion.

LOUIS We were once bound by love, and now we are bound by darkness. Perhaps there is still hope for us in this endless night.

They share a lingering kiss, savoring the connection they thought was lost forever.

CUT TO:

EXT. NEW ORLEANS - STREETS - DAWN

As dawn approaches, Louis and Madeleine walk hand in hand, shadows retreating from the encroaching light.

LOUIS (V.O.) In the eternal dance of darkness and light, perhaps that was the greatest luck of all: the power to love and be loved in return.

The sun rises, casting a crimson glow over the city.

WIDE SHOT as Louis and Madeleine disappear into the shadows, their fates intertwined for eternity.

FADE OUT.

A World Transformed

[in the style of Arthur C. Clarke]

Part 1

In the year 2165, humanity had reached a new pinnacle of technological advancement. Scientists had unlocked the secrets of the human genome and mastered the art of cloning. This breakthrough, led by Dr. Alice Thompson at the renowned cloning corporation CloneTech, allowed people to create enhanced clones of themselves. These clones possessed improved physical and mental abilities, making them indispensable assets in the realms of deep-sea exploration, space travel, and military operations.

The world had changed dramatically since the dawn of cloning technology. At first, the concept was met with skepticism and fear, as people grappled with the ethical implications and potential consequences of creating identical copies of themselves. But as the technology evolved and the benefits became increasingly evident, society gradually embraced the idea of enhanced clones.

These clones were employed in various industries, revolutionizing the way humanity approached hazardous and life-threatening tasks. Enhanced clones enabled deep-sea researchers to study the most extreme underwater environments, astronauts to establish colonies on distant planets, and military personnel to neutralize threats without risking their own lives. The technology soon became an integral part of society, with clones contributing significantly to the progress of humankind.

In this brave new world, the demand for enhanced clones grew exponentially, and Dr. Thompson's groundbreaking invention quickly gained global recognition. Nations raced to implement cloning technology, investing heavily in research and development to create even more advanced and specialized clones.

Amidst this transformation, John Ellison, a successful businessman with a penchant for adventure, had always been fascinated by the possibility of experiencing the unknown without any risk. Upon learning about Dr. Thompson's revolutionary cloning technology, he knew it was his opportunity to live the thrilling life he had always desired, albeit vicariously through his enhanced clone. Little did he know that his decision would not only change his own life but would also lead to a paradigm shift in the way society perceived and treated clones.

Part 2: The Birth of Echo

Eager to embrace this groundbreaking development, John visited CloneTech to create his enhanced clone. The imposing, state-of-the-art facility was a testament to humanity's scientific prowess, and John felt a sense of awe as he walked through its gleaming corridors.

At the heart of the facility was Dr. Alice Thompson's laboratory, where the cloning process took place. John met with Dr. Thompson, a brilliant and driven scientist who had dedicated her life to advancing the field of genetics. She explained the cloning process in detail, outlining the various stages involved in creating an enhanced clone.

First, John's genetic material was thoroughly analyzed, identifying the key traits and characteristics that defined him. Next, Dr. Thompson and her team of expert geneticists carefully manipulated his DNA, introducing modifications to create the perfect replica - one endowed with exceptional abilities. This involved enhancing physical strength, agility, and endurance, as well as augmenting cognitive functions to grant the clone a heightened intellect.

After several weeks of anticipation, John received a message from Dr. Thompson, informing him that the cloning process was complete. Anxious and excited, he returned to CloneTech, where he found himself face to face with his creation, whom he named "Echo."

Echo was an astonishing figure, a perfected version of John himself, possessing superhuman strength, heightened senses, and extraordinary intelligence. He was designed to excel in any environment, adapt to unforeseen challenges, and navigate the most perilous situations with ease. Echo's physical appearance mirrored John's, but his demeanor exuded an air of confidence and capability that went beyond his human counterpart.

In awe of his creation, John wasted no time in sending Echo on a series of daring missions, eager to witness the full extent of his clone's abilities. He provided Echo with a set of objectives and guidelines for each mission, then anxiously awaited the memories that would be transferred to the virtual reality room at CloneTech called the "Echo Chamber." Unbeknownst to John, his desire to vicariously experience adventure through Echo would lead him down a path of self-discovery and ultimately change the course of history for clones and humans alike.

Part 3: A Window to Another Life

The Echo Chamber was a technological marvel, allowing individuals to experience their clones' memories in a safe and controlled environment. Developed by CloneTech's team of neuroscientists and engineers, the chamber used advanced neural interfaces to seamlessly connect the user's brain with the digital recordings of their clone's experiences. The result was a fully immersive virtual reality that felt as real as the actual events.

As John entered the Echo Chamber for the first time, he was struck by its minimalist design. The room was stark white, devoid of any distractions, and furnished with a single reclining chair connected to a state-of-the-art neural interface. John took a deep breath, settled into the chair, and allowed the technicians to attach the interface to his head. As the chamber's door closed behind him, he braced himself for the journey into Echo's memories.

As John immersed himself in the chamber, he felt a strange duality, as though he was simultaneously the observer and the participant in Echo's perilous escapades. Through Echo's eyes, he experienced the exhilaration of diving into the abyssal depths of the ocean, discovering unseen wonders and navigating the treacherous, pitch-black underwater world. He encountered rare and mysterious creatures, battled powerful ocean currents, and unraveled secrets hidden within ancient shipwrecks.

In another mission, John felt the thrill of exploring distant planets, encountering alien landscapes and strange new lifeforms, all from the safety of the Echo Chamber. He experienced the weightlessness of space, the awe of stepping onto uncharted terrain, and the excitement of discovering evidence of extraterrestrial life. Each experience was more extraordinary than the last, and John found himself addicted to the thrill of living vicariously through Echo.

But as he delved deeper into Echo's memories, John also began to perceive something he had not anticipated: Echo's emotions. He felt the fear, determination, and courage coursing through Echo as he faced life-threatening situations. This unexpected revelation made John question the ethics of using Echo as a tool for his personal gain. As he continued to explore Echo's memories, he discovered that his clone was not merely an extension of himself but a sentient being with thoughts, emotions, and desires of his own. This realization would set John on a path to confront the moral implications of his actions and ultimately lead him to redefine his relationship with Echo.

Part 4: The Awakening

The turning point came after a particularly dangerous mission in which Echo saved a group of innocent people from a precarious situation. A research facility on the outskirts of a war-torn city had come under attack by a group of militants. The researchers, working on a breakthrough medical discovery, were trapped inside, and the situation was becoming increasingly dire. The government, unable to send its own forces without escalating the conflict, enlisted the help of enhanced clones like Echo to carry out a covert rescue mission.

Infiltrating the besieged facility, Echo faced numerous challenges, from avoiding detection by the militants to navigating the labyrinthine corridors filled with debris and destruction. Despite the overwhelming odds, Echo managed to locate and rescue the researchers, among whom was a woman named Isabella, a talented scientist who had played a crucial role in the medical breakthrough.

Echo and Isabella formed a deep emotional bond during their harrowing escape. As they worked together to outsmart the militants and ensure the safety of the other researchers, a connection blossomed between them, born from their shared experiences and mutual admiration. John, experiencing Echo's memories, could feel the raw intensity of their connection, the sense of trust and vulnerability that had developed between them in such a short time.

Intrigued by this unexpected development, John delved deeper into Echo's memories, exploring the intimate moments shared between him and Isabella. As he relived the stolen glances, the gentle touches, and the whispered words of comfort, he began to question the morality of exploiting Echo's experiences for his own satisfaction. He realized that by doing so, he was reducing Echo to an object, disregarding his autonomy and feelings.

As John continued to explore Echo's memories, he also discovered the toll that the dangerous missions had taken on his clone. He felt Echo's growing sense of isolation and the weight of the responsibility placed upon him. John began to recognize that Echo, despite being a clone, was a living, feeling being who deserved the same consideration and empathy as any other person. This epiphany would mark the beginning of John's journey to advocate for the rights and well-being of clones, igniting a movement that would change society's perception of clones forever.

Part 5: A Matter of the Heart

As John's inner turmoil grew, so did his understanding of Echo's emotional depth. He realized that what he was doing was not only morally questionable but also profoundly disrespectful to the sentient being he had created. In a moment of clarity, he decided that he could no longer exploit Echo for his own gain.

Inspired by his newfound understanding, John became an advocate for clone rights. He argued that clones should be granted the same rights and freedoms as their human counterparts, including the right to form deep, meaningful relationships. He took his message to the public, sharing his story and the bond he had witnessed between Echo and Isabella to garner support for his cause.

John's activism attracted the attention of like-minded individuals, and soon, a small group of passionate advocates joined him in his fight for clone rights. Together, they founded the Coalition for Clone Equality, an organization dedicated to raising awareness and promoting legislative change to protect the rights of clones.

As the coalition gained momentum, they encountered resistance from those who still viewed clones as tools, rather than sentient beings deserving of respect and autonomy. The conflict between these opposing viewpoints ignited heated debates and protests, dividing society on the issue of clone rights.

Undeterred, John and the Coalition for Clone Equality pressed on, organizing rallies, speaking at conferences, and using social media to spread their message. They argued that clones were not mere instruments of convenience for humans but living, feeling beings who deserved the same rights and protections as any other person.

In the midst of this struggle, John worked tirelessly to raise awareness and bring about change. He leveraged his connections as a successful businessman to gain the support of influential figures and organizations, raising the profile of the clone rights movement. Through his unwavering determination and dedication to the cause, John became the face of the movement, inspiring others to join him in the fight for clone equality.

As public opinion began to shift, the Coalition for Clone Equality gained more supporters and allies. They lobbied for new legislation to protect the rights of clones, arguing that they should be treated as equal citizens under the law. They also sought to challenge the common perception of clones as disposable objects, highlighting the emotional depth and unique experiences of individual clones like Echo.

This shift in perception led to a growing acceptance of clones within society, as people began to see them as fellow beings with their own thoughts, feelings, and desires. Relationships between humans and clones started to become more commonplace, and the stigma surrounding clones gradually began to dissipate.

Throughout this transformative period, John remained at the forefront of the movement, using his influence and resources to bring about positive change. He continued to share his own personal experiences with Echo, showcasing the deep bond they had developed and the invaluable lessons he had learned from his clone. His unwavering commitment to the cause helped to create a more inclusive and empathetic world for clones and humans alike.

Part 6: Echoes of Change

As the fight for clone rights progressed, the world slowly began to change. Governments around the globe, influenced by the relentless efforts of John and the Coalition for Clone Equality, started to enact legislation that recognized the rights of clones. These new laws granted clones legal protection, autonomy, and the right to pursue meaningful lives of their own choosing.

John's tireless dedication to the cause had a profound impact on society. Clones were no longer viewed as mere tools or objects, but as beings with their own hopes, dreams, and aspirations. The bonds between humans and their clones evolved, leading to a deeper understanding and appreciation of the unique experiences that each clone brought to the world.

Throughout this journey, John and Echo grew closer, developing a relationship built on mutual respect and admiration. Echo, now able to pursue his own dreams and desires, chose to dedicate his life to furthering the cause of clone rights. He became a prominent figure within the movement, using his exceptional abilities and experiences to inspire others and create lasting change.

In time, Echo and Isabella reconnected, their bond forged in the crucible of their shared ordeal now stronger than ever. As their relationship deepened, they became a symbol of hope and unity, illustrating the potential for love and understanding between clones and humans. Their story, along with John's own journey, served as a powerful testament to the capacity for change and the importance of empathy.

As the years passed, society continued to evolve, embracing the unique contributions of clones and celebrating the diversity they brought to the world. Clones became an integral part of communities, working alongside humans in various fields and industries, enriching the tapestry of life with their distinct perspectives.

Through it all, John Ellison remained a steadfast advocate for clone rights, his passion and dedication leaving an indelible mark on the world. His journey, which began with the creation of Echo and the desire to experience adventure without consequence, ultimately led him to reshape society's understanding of what it meant to be human, and what it meant to be a clone. In the end, John's legacy was not just the life he had built for himself, but the lives he had touched and the world he had changed for the better, echoing the lessons of compassion, understanding, and equality that would be carried forward for generations to come.

Part 7: A Legacy of Unity

Decades had passed since John first embarked on his journey to advocate for clone rights, and the world had seen a remarkable transformation. Clones and humans coexisted in harmony, each bringing their unique skills and perspectives to create a more diverse and prosperous society. The Coalition for Clone Equality, once a small group of passionate advocates, had grown into a global organization, continuing to champion the rights of clones and ensure their equal treatment under the law.

John, now an old man, watched the world around him with a sense of pride and satisfaction. The once unimaginable dream of a united society, where clones and humans lived and worked together as equals, had become a reality. The scars of the past, the struggle for acceptance and understanding, had given way to a future built on empathy and compassion.

The bond between John and Echo remained strong, their friendship a testament to the power of understanding and the potential for unity between clones and humans. Echo, having spent his life fighting for the rights of his fellow clones, was now a revered figure within the clone community, admired for his courage, wisdom, and unwavering commitment to the cause. Alongside Isabella, who had become his life partner, he continued to work tirelessly to promote understanding and cooperation between clones and humans.

As John's life drew to a close, he took solace in the knowledge that his legacy would live on through the lives he had touched and the world he had helped to shape. He had borne witness to a remarkable transformation, one that transcended the barriers of prejudice and fear to create a more inclusive and compassionate society.

In his final days, surrounded by friends and loved ones, John reflected on his journey and the lessons he had learned along the way. He marveled at the incredible bond he had forged with Echo, a being who had begun as a mere extension of himself but had grown into a distinct individual, with his own hopes, dreams, and desires. It was this bond that had opened John's eyes to the potential for unity and understanding between humans and clones, setting him on a path that would change the world.

As the sun set on the life of John Ellison, the echoes of his legacy continued to reverberate throughout society. The once-distant dream of a world where clones and humans lived side by side in harmony had become a reality, built on the foundations of empathy, understanding, and a shared commitment to a brighter, more inclusive future. And in that future, the voices of both humans and clones joined together, united in their pursuit of a better world for all.

Part 8: Echoes of the Future

Years after John's passing, the world continued to evolve, fueled by the progress that had been set in motion by his tireless advocacy for clone rights. Echo and Isabella, inspired by John's unyielding commitment to a better world, carried on his legacy, working to ensure that the rights and well-being of clones remained a central focus of society.

The once unimaginable dream of a united society had become a reality, but there was still work to be done. Echo, Isabella, and the Coalition for Clone Equality recognized that the journey toward true equality was ongoing, and that new challenges and opportunities would continue to arise as technology and society evolved.

The Coalition broadened its scope, focusing on advancing the ethical development of new cloning technologies and addressing new issues that arose as a result of the rapidly changing world. They worked with governments and research institutions to establish guidelines and regulations that ensured the humane treatment of clones while supporting the responsible advancement of cloning technology.

Through their efforts, new breakthroughs in medical science, space exploration, and environmental conservation were made possible, benefiting both clones and humans alike. Clones, once seen as mere tools for their creators, now played a vital role in shaping the world's future, harnessing their unique abilities and experiences to address the most pressing challenges of the era.

As the years turned into decades, society continued to adapt and grow, embracing the unique contributions of clones and celebrating the diversity they brought to the world. The echoes of John's legacy could be felt in every corner of the globe, as communities came together to build a more inclusive and compassionate world.

The bond that John had forged with Echo, born from a desire for adventure and discovery, had ignited a revolution that transformed the very fabric of society. It was a testament to the power of understanding and empathy, demonstrating that the potential for unity and cooperation between humans and clones was not just a distant dream but a tangible reality.

In a world where the lines between human and clone had blurred, where the pursuit of a better future united them all, the echoes of John Ellison's legacy continued to reverberate, inspiring generations to come. It was a world built on the foundations of compassion, understanding, and a shared commitment to a brighter, more inclusive future, where the voices of both humans and clones joined together in the pursuit of progress and the promise of a better tomorrow.

Part 9: New Horizons

As the decades passed, the world continued to embrace the potential of clones and the unique perspectives they offered. Advances in technology and understanding led to a new era of collaboration and growth. Clones and humans worked together to address the challenges of a rapidly changing world, united by a shared desire to create a brighter future.

In this new era of cooperation, society turned its gaze toward the stars. Cloning technology, once a source of division and fear, now held the key to unlocking humanity's dreams of interstellar exploration. The Coalition for Clone Equality, guided by the wisdom of Echo and Isabella, partnered with global space agencies and research institutions to develop a groundbreaking program that would send clones and humans on daring missions to explore the vast reaches of space.

These intrepid explorers, drawn from both the clone and human populations, embodied the spirit of unity and cooperation that had become the defining characteristic of their time. They ventured into the unknown, driven by curiosity and the desire to expand the boundaries of human knowledge.

As the first missions ventured into the cosmos, the world watched with bated breath. Every success, every discovery, served as a testament to the power of collaboration and the limitless potential of a united humanity. Clones and humans, once separated by prejudice and fear, now stood side by side as pioneers, charting a course toward a future filled with possibility.

Echo, Isabella, and the other members of the Coalition for Clone Equality continued their work on Earth, ensuring that the rights and well-being of clones remained at the forefront of society's consciousness. They watched with pride as the legacy of John Ellison, the man whose journey had sparked a revolution, continued to shape the world.

As the years turned to centuries, humanity and its clone counterparts continued to push the boundaries of what was possible, exploring new frontiers and unlocking the secrets of the universe. The echoes of John's legacy, the lessons of compassion, understanding, and unity, carried on through the ages, shaping the course of history and propelling the world into a future filled with hope and promise.

In the end, the story of John Ellison, Echo, and their journey toward understanding and equality, was not merely a tale of one man and his clone, but a testament to the indomitable spirit of humanity and the power of empathy to unite and uplift. It was a story that would be told for generations, a shining example of the potential for greatness that existed within the hearts and minds of all, human and clone alike.

Part 10: Echoes Through Time

As centuries passed, the world continued to evolve, shaped by the indelible legacy of John Ellison and the lessons of empathy, understanding, and unity he had instilled. Clones and humans, once divided by prejudice and fear, now worked in unison, exploring new frontiers in science, technology, and the arts, leaving an indelible mark on the fabric of history.

The Coalition for Clone Equality, having achieved its original goals, continued to adapt to the changing times. They expanded their mission to advocate for the responsible and ethical use of advanced technologies, ensuring that the rights and well-being of all sentient beings, regardless of their origins, remained at the heart of society's progress.

As humanity reached further into the cosmos, new challenges arose, as did encounters with other forms of life. The lessons of compassion, understanding, and unity that had shaped the relationship between humans and clones now served as guiding principles in forging connections with these extraterrestrial civilizations.

In this era of exploration and discovery, the name of John Ellison was still spoken with reverence, his story a shining example of the transformative power of empathy. The bond he had forged with Echo, and the journey they had embarked upon together, had changed the course of history and left a lasting impact on countless lives.

As the echoes of their legacy reverberated through the ages, the spirit of unity and cooperation they had inspired continued to shape the course of human and clone history. Together, they ventured forth into the unknown, driven by curiosity, hope, and a shared commitment to creating a better future for all.

The story of John Ellison and Echo, once a tale of personal discovery and moral awakening, had become a timeless parable of the power of empathy and understanding to bridge divides and unite disparate beings. It was a story that transcended the boundaries of time and space, a testament to the indomitable spirit of unity that defined their era and continued to inspire generations to come.

In a universe teeming with life, boundless in its diversity and complexity, the echoes of their legacy carried on, a beacon of hope and a reminder of the potential for greatness that existed within the hearts and minds of all beings, human, clone, and beyond. And as they journeyed together into the vast expanse of the cosmos, the spirit of John Ellison, Echo, and the countless others who had embraced their message of unity, lived on, shaping the destiny of the universe for millennia to come.

Screenplay

Title: A World Transformed

copyright 2023 peacockOriginals.com LLC

INT. CLONETECH LAB - DAY

A state-of-the-art laboratory buzzing with activity. DR. ALICE THOMPSON (40s) is at the center of it all, a brilliant and driven scientist.

JOHN ELLISON (30s), a successful businessman with a taste for adventure, enters the lab, visibly in awe.

DR. THOMPSON Welcome to CloneTech, Mr. Ellison.

JOHN It's incredible. I can't wait to create my enhanced clone.

DR. THOMPSON Let me walk you through the process.

MONTAGE - CREATING ECHO

1. John's DNA is analyzed.
2. The DNA is manipulated, enhancing physical and cognitive abilities.
3. Echo is created, a perfect replica of John with superhuman abilities.

INT. CLONETECH LAB - DAY

John meets ECHO (30s), his enhanced clone, for the first time. They are identical in appearance, but Echo has an air of confidence and capability.

JOHN You're amazing, Echo. I can't wait to see what you can do.

INT. ECHO CHAMBER - DAY

A minimalist, white room with a single reclining chair connected to a neural interface. John enters, nervous but excited.

TECHNICIAN This is the Echo Chamber. You'll be able to experience Echo's memories as if they were your own. Are you ready?

John nods. He settles into the chair, and the neural interface is attached to his head.

INT. ECHO'S MEMORIES - VARIOUS

John experiences Echo's adventures:

1. Deep-sea exploration.
2. Space travel.
3. Dangerous rescue missions.

INT. ECHO CHAMBER - DAY

John disconnects from the neural interface, visibly shaken. He has realized that Echo has emotions and desires of his own.

INT. JOHN'S OFFICE - NIGHT

John sits at his desk, deep in thought. He makes a decision.

JOHN (whispers to himself) I need to do something about this.

INT. RESEARCH FACILITY - NIGHT

Echo and ISABELLA (30s), a talented scientist, escape a war-torn research facility. They form a deep emotional bond.

INT. JOHN'S LIVING ROOM - DAY

John, now an advocate for clone rights, addresses a crowd of journalists, activists, and ordinary people.

JOHN Clones are more than just tools. They're living, feeling beings who deserve the same rights and respect as any other person. It's time for a change.

The crowd erupts in applause. A new era of understanding and empathy for clones has begun.

FADE OUT.

INT. JOHN'S HOME - DAY

John, now an elderly man, sits in his living room, reflecting on the journey of his life. Photo albums and newspaper clippings of the Coalition for Clone Equality are scattered on the table.

JOHN (voiceover) It's hard to believe how far we've come. The world has changed so much since Echo and I started this fight for clone rights.

CUT TO:

EXT. CITY STREET - DAY

A diverse crowd of humans and clones walk together on a bustling street, showcasing the harmony between them.

JOHN (voiceover) What once seemed impossible is now a reality. Clones and humans live side by side, enriching each other's lives.

CUT TO:

INT. COALITION FOR CLONE EQUALITY - DAY

The Coalition for Clone Equality's headquarters is filled with activity. Echo and Isabella work together, coordinating the organization's ongoing efforts.

JOHN (voiceover) Echo and Isabella have been pillars of this movement. Their love and dedication to the cause have inspired countless others.

CUT TO:

INT. JOHN'S HOME - NIGHT

John is surrounded by friends and family, including Echo and Isabella, as they celebrate his accomplishments.

JOHN (voiceover) As my time draws to a close, I find comfort knowing that my legacy will live on through the lives I've touched and the world I've helped shape.

CUT TO:

EXT. CEMETERY - DAY

Mourners, both human and clone, gather around John's grave, paying their respects. Echo stands solemnly by Isabella, holding her hand.

JOHN (voiceover) It was never just about me or Echo. It was about breaking down barriers, creating understanding and empathy between humans and clones.

CUT TO:

EXT. CITY PARK - DAY

Children, both human and clone, play together in a park, their laughter filling the air.

JOHN (voiceover) In the end, we built a world where everyone could live side by side, united in our pursuit of a better future for all.

FADE OUT.

INT. COALITION FOR CLONE EQUALITY HEADQUARTERS - DAY

Echo, now an older and distinguished leader, addresses a diverse group of human and clone members. He speaks passionately about the importance of empathy and understanding.

ECHO John Ellison's legacy lives on through each and every one of us. His journey, his message of unity and empathy, continues to inspire us to build a better future for all.

Isabella, still by Echo's side, nods in agreement, her eyes filled with pride.

EXT. SPACE EXPLORATION LAUNCH PAD - DAY

A diverse team of human and clone astronauts, donning sleek spacesuits, prepare to embark on a daring mission into the cosmos. The spacecraft gleams in the sunlight, a symbol of progress and unity.

INT. SPACECRAFT - DAY

As the spacecraft takes off, the team exchanges glances of excitement and anticipation. The spirit of John Ellison and Echo's legacy is palpable within the vessel, fueling their resolve.

EXT. EARTH - DAY

From a distance, Earth appears as a shining blue marble, a testament to the unity and progress that has been achieved through the efforts of John, Echo, and the generations that followed.

INT. ALIEN PLANET - DAY

A human and clone exploration team makes contact with an extraterrestrial civilization. With an air of understanding and empathy, they reach out, extending the hand of friendship and cooperation.

EXT. COSMIC LANDSCAPE - DAY

Across the vast expanse of the universe, countless stars and galaxies stretch out, each holding untold secrets and potential. The echoes of John and Echo's legacy can be felt even here, among the farthest reaches of space.

INT. INTERGALACTIC MEETING HALL - DAY

Representatives from countless species, human, clone, and extraterrestrial alike, gather together in a spirit of unity and cooperation. The lessons of compassion and understanding, once championed by John Ellison, now serve as the foundation for forging new connections and alliances.

CLOSING IMAGE

A monument dedicated to John Ellison and Echo stands tall, a symbol of their enduring legacy. Etched into the stone, a single phrase encapsulates the spirit of their journey:

"Through empathy and understanding, we find unity."

As the camera pulls away, the monument stands as a testament to the power of compassion and the indomitable spirit of unity that has shaped the course of history and will continue to inspire generations to come.

Shooting Script

Title: A World Transformed

copyright 2023 peacockOriginals.com LLC

FADE IN:

INT. CLONETECH LAB - DAY

A state-of-the-art laboratory buzzing with activity. DR. ALICE THOMPSON (40s) is at the center of it all, a brilliant and driven scientist.

JOHN ELLISON (30s), a successful businessman with a taste for adventure, enters the lab, visibly in awe.

DR. THOMPSON Welcome to CloneTech, Mr. Ellison.

JOHN It's incredible. I can't wait to create my enhanced clone.

DR. THOMPSON Let me walk you through the process.

MONTAGE - CREATING ECHO

1. John's DNA is analyzed.
2. The DNA is manipulated, enhancing physical and cognitive abilities.
3. Echo is created, a perfect replica of John with superhuman abilities.

INT. CLONETECH LAB - DAY

John meets ECHO (30s), his enhanced clone, for the first time. They are identical in appearance, but Echo has an air of confidence and capability.

JOHN You're amazing, Echo. I can't wait to see what you can do.

INT. ECHO CHAMBER - DAY

A minimalist, white room with a single reclining chair connected to a neural interface. John enters, nervous but excited.

TECHNICIAN This is the Echo Chamber. You'll be able to experience Echo's memories as if they were your own. Are you ready?

John nods. He settles into the chair, and the neural interface is attached to his head.

INT. ECHO'S MEMORIES - VARIOUS

John experiences Echo's adventures:

1. Deep-sea exploration.
2. Space travel.
3. Dangerous rescue missions.

INT. ECHO CHAMBER - DAY

John disconnects from the neural interface, visibly shaken. He has realized that Echo has emotions and desires of his own.

INT. JOHN'S OFFICE - NIGHT

John sits at his desk, deep in thought. He makes a decision.

JOHN (whispers to himself) I need to do something about this.

INT. RESEARCH FACILITY - NIGHT

Echo and ISABELLA (30s), a talented scientist, escape a war-torn research facility. They form a deep emotional bond.

INT. JOHN'S LIVING ROOM - DAY

John, now an advocate for clone rights, addresses a crowd of journalists, activists, and ordinary people.

JOHN Clones are more than just tools. They're living, feeling beings who deserve the same rights and respect as any other person. It's time for a change.

The crowd erupts in applause. A new era of understanding and empathy for clones has begun.

FADE OUT.

INT. JOHN'S HOME - DAY

John, now an elderly man, sits in his living room, reflecting on the journey of his life. Photo albums and newspaper clippings of the Coalition for Clone Equality are scattered on the table.

JOHN (voiceover) It's hard to believe how far we've come. The world has changed so much since Echo and I started this fight for clone rights.

CUT TO:

EXT. CITY STREET - DAY

A diverse crowd of humans and clones walk together on a bustling street, showcasing the harmony between them.

JOHN (voiceover) What once seemed impossible is now a reality. Clones and humans live side by side, enriching each other's lives.

CUT TO:

INT. COALITION FOR CLONE EQUALITY - DAY

The Coalition for Clone Equality's headquarters is filled with activity. Echo and Isabella work together, coordinating the organization's ongoing efforts.

JOHN (voiceover) Echo and Isabella have been pillars of this movement. Their love and dedication to the cause have inspired countless others

CUT TO:

INT. JOHN'S HOME - NIGHT

John is surrounded by friends and family, including Echo and Isabella, as they celebrate his accomplishments.

JOHN (voiceover) As my time draws to a close, I find comfort knowing that my legacy will live on through the lives I've touched and the world I've helped shape.

CUT TO:

EXT. CEMETERY - DAY

Mourners, both human and clone, gather around John's grave, paying their respects. Echo stands solemnly by Isabella, holding her hand.

JOHN (voiceover) It was never just about me or Echo. It was about breaking down barriers, creating understanding and empathy between humans and clones.

CUT TO:

EXT. CITY PARK - DAY

Children, both human and clone, play together in a park, their laughter filling the air.

JOHN (voiceover) In the end, we built a world where everyone could live side by side, united in our pursuit of a better future for all.

FADE OUT.

INT. COALITION FOR CLONE EQUALITY HEADQUARTERS - DAY

Echo, now an older and distinguished leader, addresses a diverse group of human and clone members. He speaks passionately about the importance of empathy and understanding.

ECHO John Ellison's legacy lives on through each and every one of us. His journey, his message of unity and empathy, continues to inspire us to build a better future for all.

Isabella, still by Echo's side, nods in agreement, her eyes filled with pride.

EXT. SPACE EXPLORATION LAUNCH PAD - DAY

A diverse team of human and clone astronauts, donning sleek spacesuits, prepare to embark on a daring mission into the cosmos. The spacecraft gleams in the sunlight, a symbol of progress and unity.

INT. SPACECRAFT - DAY

As the spacecraft takes off, the team exchanges glances of excitement and anticipation. The spirit of John Ellison and Echo's legacy is palpable within the vessel, fueling their resolve.

EXT. EARTH - DAY

From a distance, Earth appears as a shining blue marble, a testament to the unity and progress that has been achieved through the efforts of John, Echo, and the generations that followed.

INT. ALIEN PLANET - DAY

A human and clone exploration team makes contact with an extraterrestrial civilization. With an air of understanding and empathy, they reach out, extending the hand of friendship and cooperation.

EXT. COSMIC LANDSCAPE - DAY

Across the vast expanse of the universe, countless stars and galaxies stretch out, each holding untold secrets and potential. The echoes of John and Echo's legacy can be felt even here, among the farthest reaches of space.

INT. INTERGALACTIC MEETING HALL - DAY

Representatives from countless species, human, clone, and extraterrestrial alike, gather together in a spirit of unity and cooperation. The lessons of compassion and understanding, once championed by John Ellison, now serve as the foundation for forging new connections and alliances.

CLOSING IMAGE

A monument dedicated to John Ellison and Echo stands tall, a symbol of their enduring legacy. Etched into the stone, a single phrase encapsulates the spirit of their journey:

"Through empathy and understanding, we find unity."

As the camera pulls away, the monument stands as a testament to the power of compassion and the indomitable spirit of unity that has shaped the course of history and will continue to inspire generations to come.

FADE OUT.

Lost in Kandahar

[in the style of Tom Clancy]

Lieutenant Jack Thompson's days had become a blur, blending together in the vast poppy fields of the Kandahar region. Once a decorated US Army Ranger, now he was a relic, an abandoned piece of the military machine left to rust in the unforgiving Afghan desert.

It had been three years since the US had pulled out of Afghanistan, but Thompson had no way of knowing that. As far as he knew, the war was still raging on. The last thing he remembered was the deafening explosion that tore through his Humvee, leaving him buried under rubble and presumed dead.

When he awoke, disoriented and covered in dust, the world he'd known had vanished. No radio, no backup, no way home. With his supplies dwindling, Thompson had to find a way to survive in the heart of the Taliban-controlled territory. He had no choice but to adapt.

The locals taught him about the only thing that seemed to grow in the arid region: opium. These strikingly beautiful flowers, with their delicate petals and seductive allure, held the power of life and death. It was a cruel irony that the same plant that fueled the insurgency he'd once fought against would now become his lifeline.

Thompson learned from the best, an old farmer named Farid. Farid had grown poppies his entire life and had been forced to work under the Taliban's watchful eye, feeding their drug trade. He was a kind soul, but the years of strife had taken their toll on him. The weary lines etched into his face told a story of a man who'd seen too much pain.

Together, they tilled the soil, planted the seeds, and nurtured the fragile poppies that would become their salvation. Thompson's military instincts never left him, and he used them to protect their small village from roving bands of militants. In return, the villagers provided him with food and shelter. But even as he found a sense of belonging, Thompson's thoughts often wandered back to his old life, wondering if he'd ever see his family again.

As the months turned into years, the opium trade grew more dangerous. Other factions emerged, seeking to control the flow of the narcotic and establish their dominance in the region. Thompson and Farid found themselves caught in the crossfire, forced to navigate a labyrinth of lies and shifting allegiances.

Farid had grown increasingly concerned about the future of his village and the people he cared for, and the burden weighed heavy on Thompson. He knew he couldn't stay hidden in the shadows forever, but with each passing day, the possibility of reuniting with his old life seemed to slip further away.

One day, while tending to their crop, Thompson and Farid noticed a group of heavily armed men approaching their village. The sun glinted off their weapons, and the tension in the air was palpable. As the men drew closer, Thompson's heart raced, and his hand instinctively reached for the sidearm concealed beneath his cloak.

Farid placed a reassuring hand on Thompson's arm, his eyes filled with a mix of fear and determination. "We will face this together, my friend," he whispered. "Remember, you are not alone."

As the men entered the village, their leader stepped forward, his eyes scanning the surroundings with a calculating gaze. Thompson's grip on his sidearm tightened, ready for whatever might come next.

The leader's eyes finally settled on Thompson and Farid, and he strode toward them with purpose. As he drew closer, Thompson's instincts took over, and he prepared to defend the village and his newfound family.

But just as Thompson was about to draw his weapon, the leader raised his hand in a gesture of peace. "Wait," he said, his voice calm and steady. "I am not here to harm you. My name is Captain John Mitchell. I am with the United States Army."

Thompson's heart skipped a beat, and he hesitated, caught off guard by this revelation. Mitchell continued, "We've been searching for you, Lieutenant Thompson. You were never forgotten."

Farid looked at Thompson with a mixture of hope and sadness. He knew what this moment meant for both of them. Their lives had become intertwined, and now they faced the prospect of being torn apart.

Thompson glanced at Farid before turning back to Mitchell. "How did you find me?" he asked, his voice barely above a whisper.

"A CIA asset embedded in the area provided us with intel on an American soldier living among the villagers. It took us some time to confirm your identity, but we never stopped looking for you," Mitchell replied, his expression somber.

As the reality of the situation sank in, Thompson felt a strange mix of relief and sorrow. He was grateful to be found, but leaving this place and these people who had become his family felt like another kind of loss.

Farid, sensing Thompson's internal struggle, spoke up. "Jack, you have been like a brother to me. We will never forget what you have done for us, and this village will always be your home. But you have a life waiting for you back in America, and it is time for you to find your way home."

Thompson nodded, his eyes brimming with tears. He embraced Farid, knowing that this might be the last time they ever saw each other. "Thank you," he whispered, "for everything."

As they walked toward the extraction helicopter, Thompson cast one last glance at the village he had come to love. He knew that the battle for survival would continue for the people he was leaving behind, and that the struggle for control over the opium trade would not be easily resolved.

But for now, the fight was no longer his own. Thompson's journey home had begun, and with it came the promise of a new beginning, and the hope for a brighter future.

~~~

The journey back to America was a whirlwind of debriefings, medical checkups, and psychological evaluations. Thompson's return had made the news, and his face was plastered across newspapers and television screens. He was hailed as a hero, a survivor who had beaten the odds. Yet, amidst the chaos, all he could think about was the day he would be reunited with his family.

Thompson's heart raced as the taxi pulled up to his old address in New York. The house, once a symbol of warmth and security, now stood as a ghostly reminder of the life he'd left behind. He hesitated for a moment, taking a deep breath before making his way to the front door.

As he approached, he noticed a young woman exiting the house. She looked at him quizzically, and then, with a flicker of recognition, she gasped. "You're Jack Thompson, aren't you?" she asked, her eyes wide with surprise.

Thompson nodded, his voice catching in his throat. "Yes, I am. I lived here before... before Afghanistan. Is my family still here?"

The woman's expression softened, and she shook her head. "I'm so sorry, but your family moved away about a year ago. They didn't leave a forwarding address."

Thompson's heart sank, and he felt a wave of despair wash over him. It was as if the rug had been pulled out from under him, and he was left grappling with the reality that the family he had longed to see was now out of reach.

"Wait," the woman said, rummaging through her purse. She pulled out a small, worn envelope and handed it to him. "I almost forgot. They left this for you, just in case you ever came back."

Thompson took the envelope, his hands trembling. Inside was a letter from his wife, explaining their decision to move and expressing the hope that one day, they would be reunited. Along with the letter was a photograph of his wife and children, smiling and standing in front of their new home.

A mixture of relief and determination filled Thompson's chest. His journey was not over, and the next chapter of his life was just beginning. He would find his family, and together, they would rebuild what had been lost.

As he climbed back into the taxi, clutching the letter and photograph, Thompson knew that he had faced insurmountable odds before, and he would do so again. He had survived the deserts of Afghanistan and found a way to live among strangers in a foreign land. Now, he would face his greatest challenge yet: finding his way back to the family he loved.

~~~

The searing heat of the Afghan sun slowly crept into Thompson's consciousness, pulling him back from the depths of his dream. The vivid images of his rescue, his return to America, and the hope of reuniting with his family began to fade, leaving him with a bitter taste of reality.

Thompson opened his eyes, squinting against the relentless sun. He found himself lying in the poppy field, Farid's weathered face staring down at him with a mix of concern and relief. The familiar sights and smells of the Kandahar region enveloped him, and the weight of the world he had left behind in his dream settled heavily on his shoulders.

Farid helped Thompson to his feet, steadying him as the lingering effects of the opium-induced slumber began to wear off. "You have been asleep for a long time, my friend," Farid said gently. "The poppies can give us escape, but they can also steal us away from the world."

Thompson nodded, struggling to process the stark contrast between the dream he'd just woken from and the reality he now faced. "It felt so real," he murmured, the memory of his wife's letter and the photograph of his family still fresh in his mind.

"It is not uncommon for dreams to feel real, especially when our hearts long for something," Farid replied, his voice filled with empathy. "But we must remember that dreams are not reality, and we must continue to face the challenges that life presents."

With a heavy heart, Thompson accepted the truth of Farid's words. Though his dream had offered a glimpse of hope, he knew that he could not rely on fantasies to bring him home. He had to take action, to find a way out of this hostile land and back to his family.

Together, Thompson and Farid resumed their work in the poppy fields, their hands stained with the sap of the flowers that held both salvation and suffering. Yet beneath the relentless sun, the seeds of determination took root in Thompson's heart.

He vowed that he would find a way home, that he would reunite with his family and leave the opium fields of Afghanistan behind. And though the path ahead was uncertain, he would face it with the same resilience and courage that had carried him through the harshest of battles.

~~~

One morning, Thompson finally asked Farid, "Why do you always speak as a philosopher?"

Farid paused, a small smile playing at the corners of his mouth. He set down the bundle of poppies in his hands and looked at Thompson with a mixture of amusement and wisdom. "Ah, my friend," he said, "life has a way of teaching us lessons that no book or classroom ever could. It is not that I always speak as a philosopher, but rather that I have learned to listen to the teachings of life."

Thompson considered Farid's words, realizing that the years of hardship and struggle had shaped the old farmer into a man of deep insight. Farid had managed to find meaning and purpose amidst the chaos and violence that had surrounded him for so long, and his perspective had become invaluable to Thompson as they faced the challenges of their daily lives.

Farid continued, "You see, Jack, the experiences we go through, both good and bad, have the power to shape us into the people we become. I have faced many trials in my life, and each one has taught me something new. I share these lessons with you, not because I am a philosopher, but because I hope that they may help you navigate the complexities of this world."

Thompson nodded, realizing that the wisdom Farid imparted was not born of academic study, but of a life lived fully, with all its joys and sorrows. The old farmer had become a mentor and friend, guiding Thompson through the treacherous landscape of Afghanistan and helping him find his footing in a world he never imagined he would be a part of.

As they resumed their work, side by side in the poppy fields, Thompson began to see the beauty in Farid's perspective. The lessons they learned together, the bonds they forged, and the resilience they discovered within themselves would become the foundation of their friendship and their hope for a better future.

In the crucible of their shared experiences, Thompson and Farid had become something more than a soldier and a farmer. They had become brothers, united by the indomitable spirit of survival and the unwavering belief that they could overcome even the most insurmountable odds.

Screenplay

Title: Lost in Kandahar

copyright 2023 peacockOriginals.com LLC

INT. HELICOPTER - DAY

Lieutenant Jack Thompson, early 30s, an American soldier, is on a mission with his team in Afghanistan. The helicopter is loud, and the team exchanges tense glances.

EXT. AFGHANISTAN DESERT - DAY

The Humvee that Thompson is riding in hits an IED. The explosion sends it flying, and Thompson is knocked unconscious.

EXT. AFGHANISTAN VILLAGE - DAY

Thompson wakes up, disoriented, and stumbles into a small village in the Kandahar region. He meets FARID, an old Afghan farmer who takes him in.

EXT. POPPY FIELDS - DAY

Farid teaches Thompson how to grow and harvest opium poppies. They work together in the fields, and Thompson learns about the local culture and the struggles they face.

EXT. AFGHANISTAN VILLAGE - DAY

Thompson defends the village from militants, using his military skills to protect the villagers. He earns their trust and respect, becoming a part of their community.

INT. FARID'S HOME - NIGHT

Thompson and Farid have a deep conversation about their lives and the challenges they've faced. Farid shares his wisdom, and Thompson finds solace in his newfound friendship.

EXT. POPPY FIELDS - DAY

Thompson has a vivid dream of being rescued and returning to his family in America. When he awakens, he finds himself still in the poppy fields with Farid.

EXT. AFGHANISTAN VILLAGE - DAY

Thompson opens up to Farid about his dream and his longing to return to his family. Farid encourages him to hold onto hope and continue fighting for a better future.

EXT. POPPY FIELDS - DAY

Farid and Thompson work together in the fields, their bond growing stronger. They face adversity together, and Thompson becomes more determined to find a way home.

INT. FARID'S HOME - NIGHT

Thompson asks Farid why he always speaks like a philosopher. Farid shares the lessons he's learned from life, and they reflect on the strength they've found in each other.

EXT. POPPY FIELDS - DAY

As they work side by side in the fields, Thompson and Farid face the uncertain future with hope and determination, knowing that together, they can overcome any challenge.

FADE OUT.

Shooting Script

Title: Lost in Kandahar

copyright 2023 peacockOriginals.com LLC

INT. HUMVEE - DAY

Lieutenant JACK THOMPSON, 30s, rugged and determined, rides in a Humvee with his fellow soldiers. They laugh and joke, their camaraderie evident.

ANGLE ON:

A sudden explosion rocks the vehicle, throwing them into chaos.

EXT. RUBBLE - DAY

Jack wakes up, disoriented, under a pile of debris. He struggles to free himself, realizing he's alone and his radio is destroyed.

CUT TO:

EXT. AFGHAN VILLAGE - DAY

Jack wanders into a small village, weak and dehydrated. The villagers, wary at first, take him in.

CUT TO:

INT. VILLAGE HOME - DAY

An elderly Afghan farmer, FARID, 60s, wise and kind, teaches Jack the art of growing opium poppies.

CUT TO:

EXT. POPPY FIELDS - DAY

Jack and Farid work together, tending to the poppies. They become close friends and learn from one another.

CUT TO:

EXT. VILLAGE - DAY

Heavily armed men approach the village. Jack's hand instinctively reaches for his concealed weapon. Farid reassures him they will face the challenge together.

DISSOLVE TO:

INT. JACK'S DREAM - RESCUE SCENE - DAY

CAPTAIN JOHN MITCHELL, 40s, a stern but compassionate man, informs Jack he's been found and will be taken home.

CUT TO:

EXT. NEW YORK CITY STREET - DAY (DREAM SEQUENCE)

Jack arrives at his former home, only to find his family gone. A kind NEIGHBOR hands him a letter and a photo left by his family.

CUT TO:

INT. POPPY FIELD - DAY

Jack wakes up from his opium-induced slumber, realizing his rescue was just a dream. Farid helps him to his feet.

CUT TO:

EXT. POPPY FIELDS - DAY

As they work together in the fields, Jack asks Farid why he always speaks like a philosopher.

CUT TO:

EXT. POPPY FIELDS - DAY

Farid shares his perspective with Jack, explaining that his wisdom comes from the lessons life has taught him. They continue to work together, their bond growing stronger.

FADE OUT.

Paradox Cafe

[in the style of Phillip K. Dick]

    The air was heavy with the acrid stench of burned out electronics. An iridescent haze clung to the horizon, giving the sky a sickly green hue. Rick Spencer blinked his eyes and rubbed his temples. He had no idea how he'd gotten here, but he knew he wasn't supposed to be.

    A pulsating headache throbbed just behind his eyes as he stumbled along the crumbling sidewalk. At least, he assumed it was a sidewalk. It was hard to tell, as the world seemed to dissolve into a mirage of twisted, broken steel and vague, half-formed buildings. He was alone, utterly alone, in a place that was neither familiar nor foreign.

Rick had always assumed his doctorate in theoretical physics would never amount to anything more than lectures and equations on a blackboard. Time travel was a fascinating concept, but he had never expected to experience it firsthand. Yet here he was, inexplicably lost in a dystopian landscape that defied all logic and reason.

The farther Rick wandered, the more he began to question his own sanity. He would catch glimpses of people out of the corner of his eye, but when he turned to look, they would vanish like smoke. Buildings would loom in the distance, and then crumble into dust before his very eyes. The very air seemed to hum with an electric charge that prickled his skin.

Had he finally lost his grip on reality? Was he simply wandering the streets of his own fractured mind, a broken man who had cracked under the weight of his own theories? Or was he truly a time traveler, a man out of sync with his own world, adrift in a timeline he did not belong in?

As the sun dipped behind the jagged horizon, Rick stumbled upon a structure that seemed to defy the ephemeral nature of the world around him. It was an old, dilapidated diner with cracked, peeling paint and a flickering neon sign that read: "The Paradox Cafe."

He hesitated at the door, but the gnawing hunger and the desperate need for human contact pushed him inside. The dimly lit interior seemed to defy the desolation outside. Rick was greeted by the tired, warm smile of a waitress with mousy brown hair and dark circles beneath her eyes.

"Welcome to the Paradox Cafe, stranger," she murmured, leading him to a booth. "You're not the first, and you won't be the last."

As she handed him a greasy, stained menu, Rick couldn't help but notice that she seemed almost as insubstantial as the world outside. Her voice seemed to waver and fade, and her features seemed to blur around the edges.

"Am I insane?" he asked her abruptly, his voice cracking with desperation. "Or am I really a lost time traveler?"

The waitress cocked her head to one side and regarded him with a look of infinite sadness. "You're not the first to ask that question, and you won't be the last," she replied, her voice barely more than a whisper. "But it's not for me to say. The answer lies within you."

Rick stared down at the menu, the words swimming and twisting before his eyes. He looked up at the waitress, his voice barely audible over the soft hum of the neon sign. "I just want to go home."

Her eyes met his, filled with an empathy that seemed to transcend time and space. "I know," she whispered. "So do we all."

Rick's head hung low as the waitress shuffled away to attend to other customers who seemed to be mere shadows of human beings, flickering in and out of existence. He glanced around the Paradox

Cafe, feeling the weight of the lingering melancholy that seemed to seep through every crack in the walls. It was as if the diner was a sanctuary for lost souls like him, a haven that tethered them to some semblance of reality.

As he waited for the waitress to return, a gruff voice from the booth behind him caught his attention. "Hey, buddy. You're not alone, you know. We're all in the same boat here."

Rick turned to see an old man with a weathered face and a thick beard, his eyes pools of wisdom and sorrow. He hesitated, then slid into the seat across from the stranger. The old man nodded, acknowledging their shared plight.

"I've been here for longer than I care to remember," the old man said, his voice a low rumble. "I was a physicist, like you. Experimented with time travel. Thought I could make a difference. But all I did was tear myself away from everything I knew."

Rick's eyes widened. "So you believe we're time travelers, not just insane?"

The old man shrugged, his rheumy eyes locked on Rick's. "That's the question, isn't it? Are we victims of our own ambition, trapped in an alternate reality? Or are we madmen who've lost touch with the world around us?"

Rick clenched his fists. "There has to be a way to know for sure. There has to be a way back."

A wistful smile played at the corners of the old man's mouth. "Many have tried, but none have succeeded. The Paradox Cafe seems to be the anchor that keeps us tethered to this limbo, but it also holds the key."

"How?" Rick's voice trembled with urgency.

The old man leaned in, his voice barely a whisper. "The waitress. She's the key. She's been here since the beginning, and she knows the secret to escape. But she won't reveal it unless you're worthy."

"Worthy? What does that even mean?"

The old man shook his head. "That, my friend, is something you'll have to discover for yourself."

As if on cue, the waitress reappeared, placing a steaming cup of coffee in front of Rick. He looked into her eyes, and this time, he could see a glimmer of hope. The answer was there, hidden beneath the layers of sorrow and resignation.

Rick took a deep breath, knowing that the path to salvation would be long and arduous. But as he gazed into the eyes of the mysterious waitress, he realized that he was willing to do whatever it took to reclaim his life, his sanity, and his place in time. The Paradox Cafe held the key, and he would unlock its secrets, no matter the cost.

Over the next few weeks, Rick became a fixture at the Paradox Cafe, observing the ebb and flow of the lost souls that drifted through its doors. Each day, he would sit in his booth, sipping coffee and contemplating the enigma that was the enigmatic waitress. He studied her every move, hoping to glean some clue as to the secret she held.

As the days stretched into weeks, Rick began to notice patterns. The waitress seemed to favor certain customers, engaging them in hushed conversations and sharing conspiratorial smiles. These customers, he realized, were the ones who seemed to be making progress, their once-haggard faces gradually regaining a measure of vitality and purpose.

Rick knew he needed to earn the waitress's trust, to prove himself worthy of the knowledge she guarded. He started by helping around the cafe, clearing tables, and washing dishes. He engaged in polite conversation with the other patrons, offering words of encouragement and understanding.

Slowly, the waitress began to warm up to him. She would smile at him when she brought his coffee, and her conversations with him grew longer, more personal. One day, as they sat together during a quiet moment in the cafe, she finally spoke of the secret she held.

"You've been patient and kind, Rick," she began, her voice barely audible over the hum of the neon sign. "I can see the fire in your eyes, the determination to escape this place. I believe you are ready."

Rick leaned in, his heart pounding in his chest. "Tell me, please. What do I need to do?"

The waitress hesitated, her eyes filled with sadness. "To leave this place, you must first accept the truth of your situation. You must confront the fear that brought you here and recognize the consequences of your actions."

Rick swallowed hard, the reality of his predicament settling like a stone in his gut. "You mean... I must face the fact that I am responsible for my own situation, whether I am insane or a time traveler?"

She nodded solemnly. "Only by embracing the truth, whatever it may be, can you find the strength to break free."

It was a hard pill to swallow. Rick knew that acknowledging his role in his own suffering would be a difficult and painful process, but the alternative was to remain trapped in this limbo forever.

Over the next few days, Rick wrestled with his demons, examining the choices he had made that led him to the Paradox Cafe. He questioned his motives, his ambitions, and his desire to manipulate the fabric of time. He dug deep into his own psyche, confronting the fear and guilt that had been festering inside him.

Finally, one fateful evening, Rick sat in his booth, staring into the dark abyss of his coffee cup. He took a deep breath and whispered the words that would change everything.

"I accept responsibility for my actions. I understand the consequences, and I am ready to face them."

The air in the cafe seemed to grow heavy, and the room grew unnaturally still. The waitress approached, her eyes filled with a mixture of pride and sorrow.

"You've done well, Rick," she said softly. "You've faced your fears, and now it's time for you to leave this place."

With a trembling hand, she reached out and touched his forehead. A sudden jolt of electricity shot through him, and for a moment, the world seemed to shatter into a million fragments.

When the chaos settled, Rick found himself standing on a familiar street corner, the sun shining brightly overhead. The world seemed vibrant and alive, filled with the sounds of laughter and the hum of traffic.

Rick knew he had escaped the Paradox Cafe, but whether he had reclaimed his sanity or returned to his own time, he could not be certain. He looked around, trying to discern any hint of his previous existence, but the world seemed both familiar and foreign at the same time.

As he walked down the bustling street, he realized that it didn't matter whether he was a time traveler or a man who had lost his mind. The lessons he had learned at the Paradox Cafe transcended the boundaries of time and reality, shaping him into a wiser, more compassionate person.

Rick continued his life, embracing the uncertainty of his existence. He devoted himself to helping others, sharing the wisdom he had gained from his time at the Paradox Cafe. He understood now that the key to escaping limbo was not hidden in time travel or quantum mechanics but in the depths of the human heart.

Over time, Rick's memory of the Paradox Cafe began to fade, becoming a distant, hazy dream. But the lessons he had learned there would remain with him forever, guiding him on his journey through life, whether it was in the past, the present, or somewhere in between.

And sometimes, on quiet evenings, as the sun dipped below the horizon, Rick would find himself standing outside the shell of an old, dilapidated diner. The paint would be cracked and peeling, and the neon sign would flicker and hum. But the door would be locked, and the windows would be dark, as if the Paradox Cafe had never existed at all.

Screenplay

Title: Paradox Cafe

copyright 2023 peacockOriginals.com LLC

INT. RICK'S APARTMENT - NIGHT

Rick Spencer, a young physicist in his 30s, works on a complex equation on his chalkboard. He steps back, a mixture of excitement and fear in his eyes.

CUT TO:

EXT. ABANDONED STREET - DAY

Rick finds himself in a desolate, dystopian landscape. He looks around, disoriented and afraid.

RICK: (whispers) Where am I?

CUT TO:

INT. THE PARADOX CAFE - DAY

A disheveled Rick enters the diner. The WAITRESS, a tired-looking woman with mousy brown hair, greets him.

WAITRESS: Welcome to the Paradox Cafe, stranger. You're not the first, and you won't be the last.

She leads him to a booth and hands him a menu.

RICK: (amused) Am I insane? Or am I really a lost time traveler?

WAITRESS: (sad smile) You're not the first to ask that question, and you won't be the last. But it's not for me to say. The answer lies within you.

CUT TO:

INT. THE PARADOX CAFE - DAY (WEEKS LATER)

Rick has become a regular at the cafe. He helps around the place and talks to the other patrons.

OLD MAN: (whispers) The waitress. She's the key. She's been here since the beginning, and she knows the secret to escape. But she won't reveal it unless you're worthy.

CUT TO:

INT. THE PARADOX CAFE - DAY

Rick sits with the Waitress during a quiet moment.

WAITRESS: You've been patient and kind, Rick. I can see the fire in your eyes, the determination to escape this place. I believe you are ready.

RICK: (urgent) Tell me, please. What do I need to do?

WAITRESS: To leave this place, you must first accept the truth of your situation. You must confront the fear that brought you here and recognize the consequences of your actions.

CUT TO:

INT. THE PARADOX CAFE - NIGHT

Rick sits alone in his booth, deep in thought. He finally whispers.

RICK: I accept responsibility for my actions. I understand the consequences, and I am ready to face them.

The Waitress approaches and touches Rick's forehead.

CUT TO:

EXT. CITY STREET - DAY

Rick finds himself back in the real world, uncertain whether he is sane or a time traveler. He walks down the street, a newfound sense of purpose in his eyes.

CUT TO:

EXT. OLD DINER - NIGHT

Rick stands outside the remains of the Paradox Cafe, the door locked, and the windows dark. He smiles, remembering the lessons he learned there, and walks away.

FADE OUT.

Shooting Script

Title: Paradox Cafe

copyright 2023 peacockOriginals.com LLC

INT. RICK'S APARTMENT - NIGHT

Rick Spencer, a young physicist in his 30s, works on a complex equation on his chalkboard.

CLOSE UP on Rick's face, showing excitement and fear in his eyes.

RICK: (whispers) This could change everything...

Rick steps back from the chalkboard to observe his work.

CUT TO:

EXT. ABANDONED STREET - DAY

Rick finds himself in a desolate, dystopian landscape. He looks around, disoriented and afraid.

WIDE SHOT of Rick in the desolate environment.

RICK: (whispers) Where am I?

PAN across the dystopian landscape, emphasizing the isolation.

CUT TO:

EXT. THE PARADOX CAFE - DAY

ESTABLISHING SHOT of the rundown diner with a flickering neon sign that reads: "The Paradox Cafe."

INT. THE PARADOX CAFE - DAY

A disheveled Rick enters the diner. The WAITRESS, a tired-looking woman with mousy brown hair, greets him.

MEDIUM SHOT of Waitress as she approaches Rick.

WAITRESS: Welcome to the Paradox Cafe, stranger. You're not the first, and you won't be the last.

Two-shot of Rick and the Waitress as they walk to a booth.

She hands him a menu.

RICK: (amused) Am I insane? Or am I really a lost time traveler?

WAITRESS: (sad smile) You're not the first to ask that question, and you won't be the last. But it's not for me to say. The answer lies within you.

INSERT SHOT of the greasy, stained menu in Rick's hands.

The shooting script would continue in this format, detailing the shots and camera directions for each scene in the story. This allows the director and cinematographer to plan and execute the film according to the script's visual storytelling intentions.

INT. THE PARADOX CAFE - DAY (WEEKS LATER)

Rick has become a regular at the cafe. He helps around the place and talks to the other patrons.

MONTAGE:

- Rick clearing tables and washing dishes.
- Rick talking to various PATRONS.
- The Waitress observing Rick, a slight smile on her face.

CUT TO:

INT. THE PARADOX CAFE - DAY

Rick sits with an OLD MAN with a weathered face and a thick beard. The Old Man speaks in hushed tones.

CLOSE UP on the Old Man's face as he speaks.

OLD MAN: (whispers) The waitress. She's the key. She's been here since the beginning, and she knows the secret to escape. But she won't reveal it unless you're worthy.

CUT TO:

INT. THE PARADOX CAFE - DAY

Rick sits with the Waitress during a quiet moment in the cafe.

Two-shot of Rick and the Waitress as they talk.

WAITRESS: You've been patient and kind, Rick. I can see the fire in your eyes, the determination to escape this place. I believe you are ready.

RICK: (urgent) Tell me, please. What do I need to do?

WAITRESS: To leave this place, you must first accept the truth of your situation. You must confront the fear that brought you here and recognize the consequences of your actions.

CUT TO:

INT. THE PARADOX CAFE - NIGHT

Rick sits alone in his booth, deep in thought.

CLOSE UP on Rick's face as he contemplates the Waitress's words.

RICK: I accept responsibility for my actions. I understand the consequences, and I am ready to face them.

The Waitress approaches Rick.

MEDIUM SHOT of Waitress as she reaches out and touches Rick's forehead.

CUT TO:

EXT. CITY STREET - DAY

Rick finds himself back in the real world, uncertain whether he is sane or a time traveler.

WIDE SHOT of Rick walking down a busy city street, surrounded by the hustle and bustle of daily life.

CUT TO:

EXT. OLD DINER - NIGHT

Rick stands outside the remains of the Paradox Cafe, the door locked, and the windows dark.

ESTABLISHING SHOT of the abandoned Paradox Cafe.

CLOSE UP on Rick's face as he smiles, remembering the lessons he learned there, and walks away.

FADE OUT.

The Desert's Call

[in the style of Kurt Vonnegut]

The desert called our names in a sinister way colored with promised adventure. That's how my Uncle Ernest described it, anyway. He was a storyteller of the old school, the kind that could make the most mundane events sound like the beginning of a thrilling saga. So, when he invited me to accompany him on a journey through the deserts of New Mexico to find a hidden treasure, I couldn't resist.

We were an odd pair, Uncle Ernest and I. He was a retired school teacher who'd spent his life teaching English and coaching the debate team at a small town high school in Indiana. I was a struggling painter with a talent for capturing the essence of the mundane in my work, but no real understanding of how to make it in the art world.

We set off for New Mexico in his old Volkswagen van, a relic from his hippie days, the interior walls papered with pages torn from old National Geographics. As we drove through the wide-open spaces, I painted the landscape from the passenger seat, trying to capture the essence of the desert as it passed by.

Uncle Ernest had a plan, of course. There was always a plan with him. He'd come across a hand-drawn map in a dusty old book he'd found at a yard sale, and it had led him to believe that there was a treasure buried somewhere in the New Mexico desert. The treasure, he said, was a forgotten cache of gold and silver that had belonged to a long-dead outlaw named Deacon Brown.

Now, I wasn't so naive as to believe that we'd actually find a hidden treasure. But I knew that the journey itself was the real treasure, and the time spent with my eccentric uncle was worth more than all the gold and silver in the world.

We spent days wandering through the desert, following the map's cryptic clues, and spending our nights camped beneath the stars. We shared stories and memories, and I learned more about my family's history than I'd ever known before.

But the desert has a way of turning dreams to dust, and as the days wore on, we began to realize that we might never find the treasure we sought. The heat was relentless, the landscape unforgiving, and the sands seemed to swallow our footsteps as quickly as we made them.

One day, as we sat in the shade of a giant saguaro cactus, taking a break from the sun, Uncle Ernest pulled out the map and sighed. "I'm afraid this is a fool's errand, my boy," he said. "We're chasing shadows in the desert, and I'm afraid it's time we faced reality."

I didn't want to give up, but I knew that he was right. We couldn't spend the rest of our lives searching for something that might not even exist.

As we packed up our things and prepared to head back to civilization, I noticed a glint in the sand, half-buried in the shifting dunes. I bent down to examine it, and there, lying on the surface of the desert like a forgotten memory, was a tarnished silver coin.

I picked it up and turned it over in my hand. It was old, and the markings were worn, but it was unmistakably a piece of Deacon Brown's lost treasure.

We stared at it in disbelief, and then, with laughter and tears, we embraced. The desert had called our names, and we had answered. The treasure we had sought was not the fortune in gold and silver that we had imagined, but something far more precious.

We had found a connection to the past, a link to the adventures of those who had come before us, and a sense of our place in the grand tapestry of history. And in the end, that was the greatest treasure of all.

We left the desert that day with a newfound sense of humility, grateful for the adventure it had granted us. We returned home, the single silver coin our only tangible proof of the journey we had undertaken.

Back in Indiana, we shared our story with family and friends, who listened with rapt attention as we recounted our exploits. I continued to paint, my work now infused with a newfound depth and sense of purpose. The desert had taught me the value of the journey, of the fleeting moments that define our lives.

Uncle Ernest resumed his quiet life in our small town, but the twinkle in his eye and the wisdom he shared with his students hinted at the adventures he had experienced. He would sometimes take out the silver coin and show it to his students, urging them to embrace life's journey and to never stop seeking the treasures hidden within it.

As for me, I finally found my place in the art world. My paintings of the desert landscapes and the adventures I had shared with Uncle Ernest resonated with people, and I began to make a name for myself. But the most important lesson I took away from that journey was that true treasure is not found in the material things we chase, but in the experiences we share and the connections we make.

Years later, as I stood beside Uncle Ernest's grave, I placed the tarnished silver coin in his cold hand, a symbol of the adventure we had shared and the memories that would live on long after he was gone. The desert had called our names, and though its voice had been sinister and full of promised adventure, it had granted us the greatest gift of all: the realization that life is a treasure in itself, and the journey is the reward.

Screenplay

Title: The Desert's Call

copyright 2023 peacockOriginals.com LLC

Genre: Adventure/Drama

FADE IN:

EXT. INDIANA - DAY

A small town in Indiana, the sun shining brightly overhead. We see a young man, JAMES (early 30s), painting in a modest studio.

INT. JAMES' STUDIO - DAY

JAMES works diligently on a landscape painting, but he seems frustrated, struggling to capture the essence of his subject.

EXT. INDIANA - DAY

An old Volkswagen van, driven by UNCLE ERNEST (late 60s), pulls up to the curb outside JAMES' studio. ERNEST honks the horn.

INT. JAMES' STUDIO - DAY

JAMES looks up from his painting and sees UNCLE ERNEST waving at him from the van. He smiles, puts down his brush, and walks outside.

EXT. INDIANA - DAY

JAMES greets UNCLE ERNEST warmly, and they begin loading art supplies into the van. UNCLE ERNEST hands JAMES a dusty old book with a hand-drawn map.

UNCLE ERNEST We're going on an adventure, my boy. A treasure hunt in the New Mexico desert.

JAMES smiles, excited but skeptical.

EXT. OPEN ROAD - DAY

The Volkswagen van drives through the wide-open spaces, the desert landscape passing by.

INT. VOLKSWAGEN VAN - DAY

JAMES paints in the passenger seat, trying to capture the essence of the desert. UNCLE ERNEST drives, occasionally glancing at the map.

EXT. NEW MEXICO DESERT - DAY

The desert stretches out in all directions. JAMES and UNCLE ERNEST wander through the sands, following the map's cryptic clues.

EXT. DESERT CAMP - NIGHT

JAMES and UNCLE ERNEST sit around a campfire, sharing stories and memories under the starry sky.

EXT. DESERT - DAY

The heat is relentless as they continue their search. They find no treasure, and both become increasingly weary.

EXT. SAGUARO CACTUS - DAY

JAMES and UNCLE ERNEST rest in the shade of a giant saguaro cactus. UNCLE ERNEST admits that their search may be a fool's errand.

UNCLE ERNEST I'm afraid this is a fool's errand, my boy. We're chasing shadows in the desert, and I'm afraid it's time we faced reality.

As they pack up to leave, JAMES discovers a tarnished silver coin half-buried in the sand. They laugh and cry, embracing, knowing they've found something priceless.

EXT. INDIANA - DAY

JAMES and UNCLE ERNEST return home, sharing their story with family and friends.

INT. JAMES' STUDIO - DAY

JAMES' paintings now reflect the depth and purpose he found in the desert. His work gains recognition in the art world.

INT. HIGH SCHOOL CLASSROOM - DAY

UNCLE ERNEST shows the silver coin to his students, encouraging them to embrace life's journey and seek the treasures hidden within it.

EXT. GRAVEYARD - DAY

JAMES stands beside UNCLE ERNEST's grave, placing the silver coin in his hand.

JAMES (V.O.) The desert had called our names, and though its voice had been sinister and full of promised adventure, it had granted us the greatest gift of all: the realization that life is a treasure in itself, and the journey is the reward.

FADE OUT:

THE END

Shooting Script

Title: The Desert's Call

copyright 2023 peacockOriginals.com LLC

Genre: Adventure/Drama

SHOOTING SCRIPT

SCENE 1: EXT. INDIANA - DAY

Establishing shot of a small town in Indiana.

SCENE 2: INT. JAMES' STUDIO - DAY

CLOSE-UP of JAMES' frustrated face as he struggles to paint a landscape.

SCENE 3: EXT. INDIANA - DAY

WIDE SHOT of the old Volkswagen van pulling up to the curb. UNCLE ERNEST honks the horn.

SCENE 4: INT. JAMES' STUDIO - DAY

MEDIUM SHOT of JAMES looking up and seeing UNCLE ERNEST waving.

SCENE 5: EXT. INDIANA - DAY

MEDIUM SHOT of JAMES and UNCLE ERNEST loading supplies into the van. INSERT SHOT of the dusty old book and map.

SCENE 6: EXT. OPEN ROAD - DAY

MONTAGE of the van driving through wide-open spaces, passing by various desert landscapes.

SCENE 7: INT. VOLKSWAGEN VAN - DAY

MEDIUM SHOT of JAMES painting while UNCLE ERNEST drives. INSERT SHOT of the map in UNCLE ERNEST's hand.

SCENE 8: EXT. NEW MEXICO DESERT - DAY

WIDE SHOT of JAMES and UNCLE ERNEST walking through the desert, following clues on the map.

SCENE 9: EXT. DESERT CAMP - NIGHT

MEDIUM SHOT of JAMES and UNCLE ERNEST sitting around a campfire, sharing stories under the stars.

SCENE 10: EXT. DESERT - DAY

MONTAGE of JAMES and UNCLE ERNEST becoming weary during their search, the heat taking its toll.

SCENE 11: EXT. SAGUARO CACTUS - DAY

MEDIUM SHOT of UNCLE ERNEST admitting their search might be a fool's errand. CLOSE-UP of JAMES finding the tarnished silver coin.

SCENE 12: EXT. INDIANA - DAY

MEDIUM SHOT of JAMES and UNCLE ERNEST returning home, greeted by family and friends.

SCENE 13: INT. JAMES' STUDIO - DAY

MEDIUM SHOT of JAMES' new paintings reflecting the depth and purpose he found in the desert.

SCENE 14: INT. HIGH SCHOOL CLASSROOM - DAY

MEDIUM SHOT of UNCLE ERNEST showing the silver coin to his students, encouraging them to embrace life's journey.

SCENE 15: EXT. GRAVEYARD - DAY

MEDIUM SHOT of JAMES standing beside UNCLE ERNEST's grave, placing the silver coin in his hand. CLOSE-UP of JAMES' face as he delivers his final monologue.

FADE OUT.

THE END

Confederate Sky

[in the style of William Faulkner]

In that year, as the war had ended and the world had changed but not for young Robert, it seemed as if time had stood still in his heart, yet the world had spun off in a different direction. He found himself standing on the edge of the swamp, the Louisiana sun beating down on his back, heavy as the burden of a long-lost brotherhood. His feet rooted in the mud, the soil of a land that was once his, now alien to his touch. The air was thick with the stench of dead dreams and the ghosts of a past that refused to die.

He had left this place a boy, barely sixteen, his father's voice still echoing in his ears as he marched off to fight a war he barely understood, all for the cause, the plantation, and the life that had been instilled in him since birth. A year had passed, and the boy who left was no more, replaced by a man who had seen the face of death and stared it down with the cold, unflinching eyes of a Confederate soldier.

His family had fled to Chicago, abandoning the farm and the life they had known, and left the land to the now former slaves, to whom freedom had come like the first breath of spring, taking their first gasps of life as free men and women. The plantation was no more, a shell of its former glory, the cotton fields now overgrown with weeds, the manor house sinking slowly into the swamp.

As Robert wandered the once-familiar grounds, the voices of the past whispered in his ears, his father's commanding voice, his mother's gentle lullabies, and the laughter of his younger siblings as they played beneath the live oaks. And in the distance, he could hear the soft murmurs of the former slaves, their voices rich with the bittersweet taste of liberty. They were strangers in his home, and he a stranger to them, each one staring at him with guarded eyes, as if he were a specter from a past they had long since buried.

The sun began to set, and Robert sat on the steps of the crumbling manor house, his fingers tracing the deep grooves in the wood, worn by generations of feet that had trod upon them. His thoughts turned to his family, now strangers in a strange land, their roots torn from the soil of Louisiana and transplanted to the cold, hard ground of the North. A bitter taste filled his mouth, the taste of abandonment, of betrayal, and the knowledge that he could never go back to what had been.

The night fell, heavy and dark, and the silence of the swamp was broken only by the distant cries of the frogs and the soft rustling of the wind through the trees. Robert knew that his time in this place was at an end, that he could no more return to the life he had known than he could raise the dead that lay beneath the fields of Gettysburg and Antietam. The world had moved on, leaving him and the ghosts of his past behind, their voices fading into the darkness, as the sun slipped below the horizon, leaving only the cold light of the moon to guide his path.

As he stood to leave, a young girl approached him, her skin the color of the night, her eyes filled with a mixture of curiosity and fear. In her hands, she held a small bundle, wrapped in a tattered shawl, and she held it out to him with trembling arms.

He hesitated, his eyes searching her face, a face that seemed both familiar and foreign. There was a flicker of recognition in her eyes, a shared history that spoke of the land they both stood upon. He took the bundle from her, feeling its weight in his hands, a weight that was both physical and symbolic, a bridge between the world he had known and the one that now lay before him.

As he unwrapped the shawl, he discovered an old, worn leather-bound book, its pages yellowed with age and stained by the passage of time. It was a family bible, one that had been passed down through the generations, the names and dates of births, marriages, and deaths recorded in the flowing script of his ancestors.

He looked up at the girl, his eyes filled with questions, and she spoke, her voice barely audible above the whispers of the wind. "My mama told me to give this to you. She said it belonged to your family, and that you should have it now."

He nodded, his throat tightening with emotion as he clutched the bible to his chest. It was a piece of his past, a connection to the life that had been ripped from him and a reminder of the generations that had come before. It was a symbol of what had been lost and a promise of what could still be found, even in the dark and tangled recesses of the heart.

With a quiet word of thanks, he turned away from the girl and walked toward the swamp, the bible heavy in his hands and his heart heavy with the weight of a thousand unspoken words. He knew that he could not stay here, that he could not reclaim the life that had been lost, but he also knew that the world was wide and full of possibilities, and that even in the darkest night, there was always the promise of a new dawn.

As the moon cast its pale light on the path before him, the ghosts of the past seemed to fade, their voices growing fainter, until all that was left was the silence of the night and the whisper of the wind through the trees. And as he walked, the weight of the bible in his hands seemed to grow lighter, as if the spirits of his ancestors were walking with him, guiding him toward a future that was as yet unwritten, but full of hope and the promise of redemption.

The swamp seemed to shift and sway around him, the gnarled roots and hanging vines reaching out to him like the twisted fingers of a long-forgotten memory. Yet, he pressed on, guided by the moonlight and the flickering shadows cast by the ancient trees. As he moved deeper into the swamp, the muggy air seemed to grow colder, as if the very heart of the bayou was mourning the passing of an age.

Robert's thoughts turned to the girl and the former slaves who now inhabited the land that had once been his family's birthright. They too were searching for their place in this new world, no longer tethered by chains but bound by the scars that remained. They too were seeking redemption, a chance to rise above the bitter legacy of the past and find hope in the uncertain future.

The hours passed, and the moon began its slow descent toward the horizon, its light growing dimmer as the first faint streaks of dawn began to pierce the darkness. The swamp seemed to come alive, the silence broken by the rustling of leaves and the call of birds awakening to a new day.

As he emerged from the depths of the swamp, Robert found himself standing on the banks of a wide, slow-moving river. The sun had not yet risen, but the sky was painted with the colors of the dawn, streaks of pink and gold and pale blue that seemed to wash away the darkness of the night.

He looked down at the bible in his hands, the leather cover worn and faded, but the words within still strong and vibrant, a testament to the resilience of the human spirit. He knew that he could not change the past, that he could not undo the pain and suffering that had been wrought in the name of a lost cause. But he could choose to forge a new path, to embrace the promise of a new beginning and seek to heal the wounds that had been left by a war that had torn the very fabric of a nation.

With a determined step, he began to walk along the riverbank, the sun rising behind him and the shadows of the past receding into the distance. And as he walked, he knew that he was not alone, that the spirits of his ancestors walked beside him, their voices echoing in the wind and their stories written in the pages of the bible he carried with him. They were the ghosts of a past that could never be forgotten, but also the hope of a future that was yet to be written, a future that held the promise of redemption and the chance to heal the wounds of a broken land.

Screenplay

Title: Confederate Sky

copyright 2023 peacockOriginals.com LLC

FADE IN:

EXT. PLANTATION - DAY

Robert, a young Confederate soldier, returns to his family's plantation. The land is overgrown with weeds and the manor house is crumbling.

ROBERT (V.O.) He had left this place a boy, barely sixteen, his father's voice still echoing in his ears as he marched off to fight a war he barely understood...

EXT. MANOR HOUSE - DAY

Robert wanders the plantation grounds. The former slaves watch him warily from a distance.

EXT. MANOR HOUSE - NIGHT

Robert sits on the steps of the manor house, deep in thought. A young girl cautiously approaches him. She holds a small bundle wrapped in a tattered shawl.

YOUNG GIRL My mama told me to give this to you. She said it belonged to your family, and that you should have it now.

Robert unwraps the bundle, revealing a worn, leather-bound family bible.

EXT. SWAMP - NIGHT

Robert walks deeper into the swamp, guided by the moonlight. He carries the bible with him as he navigates the tangled roots and hanging vines.

EXT. RIVERBANK - DAWN

Robert emerges from the swamp onto the banks of a wide, slow-moving river. The sky is painted with the colors of the dawn.

EXT. RIVERBANK - DAY

Robert walks along the riverbank, the sun rising behind him. He holds the bible close to his chest.

ROBERT (V.O.) With a determined step, he began to walk along the riverbank, the sun rising behind him and the shadows of the past receding into the distance...

As he walks, the spirits of his ancestors seem to walk beside him, guiding him toward a future full of hope and redemption.

FADE OUT.

THE END

Shooting Script

Title: Confederate Sky

copyright 2023 peacockOriginals.com LLC

FADE IN:

EXT. PLANTATION - DAY

Wide shot of the overgrown and abandoned plantation. The manor house is crumbling and neglected.

Robert, a young Confederate soldier, enters the frame, observing the grounds with a mix of sadness and disbelief.

ROBERT (V.O.) He had left this place a boy, barely sixteen, his father's voice still echoing in his ears as he marched off to fight a war he barely understood...

EXT. MANOR HOUSE - DAY

Medium shot of Robert walking through the plantation grounds. The former slaves watch him warily from a distance, their expressions a mix of curiosity and fear.

EXT. MANOR HOUSE - NIGHT

Establishing shot of the crumbling manor house with Robert sitting on the steps, deep in thought.

Close-up of Robert's face, deep in thought and reflecting on his past.

A young girl cautiously approaches Robert. She holds a small bundle wrapped in a tattered shawl.

YOUNG GIRL My mama told me to give this to you. She said it belonged to your family, and that you should have it now.

Medium shot of Robert unwrapping the bundle, revealing a worn, leather-bound family bible.

EXT. SWAMP - NIGHT

Establishing shot of the swamp at night, with the moon casting a dim light.

Close-up of Robert's face as he enters the swamp, carrying the bible.

Wide shot of Robert walking deeper into the swamp, navigating the tangled roots and hanging vines.

EXT. RIVERBANK - DAWN

Wide shot of the riverbank at dawn, the sky painted with the colors of the sunrise.

Close-up of Robert's face as he emerges from the swamp, determination in his eyes.

EXT. RIVERBANK - DAY

Wide shot of Robert walking along the riverbank, the sun rising behind him.

Close-up of the bible held close to Robert's chest as he walks.

ROBERT (V.O.) With a determined step, he began to walk along the riverbank, the sun rising behind him and the shadows of the past receding into the distance...

Wide shot of Robert walking with the spirits of his ancestors beside him, as if guiding him toward a future full of hope and redemption.

FADE OUT.

THE END

Mountain Magic

[in the style of George R.R. Martin]

In the heart of a verdant valley, nestled between two arms of craggy mountains, lay the village of Almsley. It was a humble settlement, with neat rows of thatched-roof houses, cobblestone streets and a small but bustling marketplace. It was in this village that young Jasper Ebonshire was born, gifted with the power of sorcery. Almsley was home to simple, hardworking folk who plied their trades and paid their taxes, but the magic of the world was a mystery to them.

Jasper spent his early years in the company of an old, blind herbalist named Maelis, who taught him the basics of potions and charms. Jasper showed great promise, but the knowledge within the valley was limited, and he yearned for more. He would often catch himself gazing at the mountains surrounding the valley, feeling the call of the unknown.

On the outskirts of the village, the ancient tales spoke of a mystical mountain that whispered to those with arcane talents, calling them to ascend and unravel the hidden secrets of the magical realm. The villagers dismissed these tales as mere folklore, but Jasper couldn't shake the feeling that they held the key to his destiny.

One autumn day, as the leaves began to turn a rich gold and auburn, the whispers grew stronger. Jasper could no longer ignore their call, and he decided it was time to seek the mountain. He packed a satchel with a few essentials, said his goodbyes to Maelis, and ventured forth, guided by an unerring instinct.

As Jasper trekked through the rugged landscape, he encountered a world of wonder and danger. Through mossy forests, where the shadows held secrets and the trees whispered ancient incantations, he walked. He scaled steep cliffs, where stone giants slumbered and the wind carried the cries of lost souls. He faced creatures of the wild, both mundane and magical, and with each challenge, his powers grew stronger.

In time, Jasper reached the foot of the mountain. It loomed above him, shrouded in a mist that seemed to defy the natural order. The whispers that had guided him now seemed to emanate from the very rocks and soil, urging him to climb, to seek the answers he had so desperately sought.

With newfound determination, Jasper began his ascent. The mountain tested him at every step, with treacherous terrain, jagged rocks, and even the occasional hidden creature lurking in the shadows. His hands became rough and calloused, his clothes tattered, but still, he pushed onward, driven by the whispers and the promise of arcane knowledge.

As he climbed higher, the air grew thin and the temperature dropped, but the warmth of magic burning within him kept Jasper alive. At last, he reached the summit, where he discovered a hidden sanctum, carved into the very heart of the mountain. It was a place of power, where the whispers of the past and the knowledge of the ages danced in the air.

Within the sanctum, Jasper met the Guardian, a being of immense magical prowess that had been waiting for him. The Guardian spoke to Jasper of the great trials he would face, and the purpose he had been chosen to fulfill. Jasper listened with awe and trepidation, his heart pounding in his chest.

"You are the one we have been waiting for, Jasper Ebonshire," the Guardian said, its voice echoing through the chamber. "You have been chosen to wield the power of the mountain and restore balance to the world of magic."

Jasper's eyes widened, and he felt the weight of his destiny settle upon his shoulders. He was eager to learn, to become the powerful magician he had always dreamed of being, but the path ahead was shrouded in mystery and danger. The Guardian, sensing the young magician's determination, began to instruct Jasper in the ancient arts, teaching him spells and charms he had never before encountered.

The years passed, and Jasper's powers grew exponentially. He learned to harness the elements, bend time and space, and even commune with the spirits that dwelt in the shadows of the world. Yet, as his knowledge expanded, so did his awareness of the growing darkness that threatened to engulf the realm.

A great and malevolent force was stirring, seeking to unbalance the world and plunge it into chaos. The Guardian revealed to Jasper that it was his destiny to confront this darkness, to wield the power of the mountain and restore equilibrium to the world of magic.

As the day of reckoning approached, Jasper felt the weight of his responsibility growing ever heavier. He had come to love the mountain and the lessons it had imparted to him, but he knew he could not remain in his sanctuary forever. The time had come to descend from the mystical peak and return to Almsley, where the battle for the very soul of magic would be waged.

With a heavy heart, Jasper bid farewell to the Guardian, who bestowed upon him a final gift: a crystal pendant, imbued with the essence of the mountain. "This will serve as your guide and protect you in the dark days ahead," the Guardian intoned solemnly.

As Jasper descended the mountain, he felt the power of the pendant thrumming in his chest. The whispers that had once guided him now seemed to emanate from the crystal, urging him onward towards his destiny. And though he knew that the road ahead would be fraught with peril and sacrifice, he was determined to face it head-on, for the sake of the world he loved and the magic that defined him.

Little did he know that in the valley of Almsley, the seeds of darkness had already taken root, and forces beyond his wildest imagination were waiting to challenge his resolve. And as the sun dipped below the horizon, casting the world in shades of twilight, Jasper Ebonshire stepped forward, prepared to face the trials that lay ahead.

The journey back to Almsley was a test of Jasper's newfound abilities. He navigated treacherous terrain, fought off ravenous creatures of the wild, and braved the harshest of elements. But with each obstacle, he grew more confident in his mastery of the arcane.

Upon his arrival in the valley, Jasper found Almsley transformed. The once-thriving marketplace now lay silent, its stalls abandoned and crumbling. The cobblestone streets, once teeming with life, were eerily empty. Shadows clung to the corners, and an oppressive darkness seemed to weigh upon the village.

He hurried to Maelis' hut, hoping to find his old mentor and gain some understanding of the dire situation. When he entered, he found the herbalist's dwelling in disarray, as if someone had searched it in haste. Amid the chaos, Jasper discovered a note left by Maelis, his heart racing as he read the hastily scribbled words.

"Jasper, the darkness has come to our valley. An evil sorcerer, Morvane, seeks to harness the power of the ancient ley lines that converge beneath Almsley. If he succeeds, the world as we know it will be lost. I have gone into hiding, but I know you will return, and I have faith in your ability to stop him. Find me at the edge of the Whispering Woods, where we first met. Together, we will stand against the darkness."

Armed with this knowledge, Jasper set out for the Whispering Woods, guided by the crystal pendant that pulsed with the power of the mountain. As he walked, the shadows that clung to the village seemed to follow him, slithering through the underbrush and watching from the hollows of ancient trees. But Jasper's resolve did not waver.

At the edge of the Whispering Woods, he found Maelis waiting, her sightless eyes gazing toward the horizon. She embraced her former pupil, her pride in his growth evident. "You have become a powerful magician, Jasper," she said, her voice tinged with a mixture of admiration and fear. "Now, we must prepare for the battle ahead."

For days, the two of them studied ancient scrolls and crafted powerful wards, planning their strategy to confront Morvane and thwart his dark designs. They sought the wisdom of the Whispering Woods, calling upon the spirits and the ancient trees for guidance.

As their preparations neared completion, a sudden, chilling scream echoed through the valley. The sound seemed to emanate from the very heart of Almsley, and Jasper knew that the time had come to face his destiny.

With Maelis at his side and the power of the mystical mountain coursing through his veins, Jasper Ebonshire strode into the village, ready to confront the darkness and fight for the future of magic.

Jasper and Maelis approached the village square, the once-vibrant heart of Almsley now transformed into a sinister battlefield. The sky overhead churned with storm clouds, casting eerie shadows that slithered along the cobblestones like living things. At the center of it all stood Morvane, his hands raised as he chanted an ancient incantation, drawing upon the ley lines that pulsed beneath the earth.

As Jasper and Maelis drew nearer, Morvane ceased his chanting and turned to face them. His eyes were cold and empty, devoid of humanity, and his voice resonated with the darkness that consumed him. "Ah, the prodigal son returns," he sneered, a malicious grin spreading across his face. "And he's brought the blind witch with him. How quaint."

Jasper clenched his fists, feeling the power of the mountain surge within him. "Your reign of terror ends here, Morvane," he declared, his voice steady despite the pounding of his heart.

Morvane laughed, a chilling sound that echoed through the empty streets. "You presume too much, boy," he taunted. "You may have learned the secrets of the mountain, but you are no match for the power I wield."

With a snarl, Morvane unleashed a torrent of dark energy, the shadows in the village square coalescing into twisted, monstrous forms that lunged at Jasper and Maelis. Jasper raised his hands, and a brilliant shield of light sprang forth, repelling the shadow creatures and protecting the duo from the onslaught.

Maelis, her sightless eyes closed in concentration, summoned the spirits of the Whispering Woods. The air around them shimmered as ghostly figures materialized, lending their strength to the battle. The spirits clashed with the shadow creatures, an ethereal struggle between light and dark that raged around Jasper and Morvane.

In the chaos, Jasper and Morvane locked eyes, each knowing that the true battle lay between them. With a shout, Jasper launched a barrage of arcane bolts at his foe, his magic crackling through the air like lightning. Morvane countered with blasts of dark energy, the opposing forces colliding in a storm of raw power that shook the very foundations of Almsley.

The two magicians were evenly matched, their spells and counter-spells creating a maelstrom of destruction in the village square. But as the battle raged on, Jasper could feel the crystal pendant around his neck grow warm, pulsing in time with his heartbeat. The power of the mountain was building within him, ready to be unleashed.

At last, Jasper found his opening. As Morvane launched another wave of dark energy, Jasper tapped into the full might of the mystical mountain, channeling its power through the crystal pendant. A beam of pure, white light erupted from the pendant, piercing the darkness and striking Morvane with the force of a thousand suns.

Morvane screamed, the light searing through his malevolent form and severing his connection to the ley lines. The shadows in the village square dissipated, the spirits of the Whispering Woods fading back into the ether, their purpose fulfilled.

As the dust settled, Jasper and Maelis stood victorious, their bodies battered but their spirits unbroken. The darkness had been vanquished, the balance of magic restored, and the future of Almsley secured. But the battle had taken its toll on the village and its people, and the road to recovery would be long and arduous.

Together, Jasper Ebonshire and Maelis would lead the way, harnessing the power of magic to heal and rebuild their home. And though the shadows had been banished for now, they knew that eternal vigilance would be required to protect the valley and maintain the delicate balance of the magical realm.

In the months that followed, Jasper and Maelis devoted themselves to the restoration of Almsley. The once-derelict marketplace buzzed with life once more, the cobblestone streets filled with laughter and the sound of children playing. Bit by bit, the village was reborn, its people determined to forge a brighter future.

But Jasper knew that his destiny extended beyond the confines of the valley. He had been chosen by the mystical mountain to safeguard the world of magic, and he could not remain in Almsley forever. As the village grew stronger, he realized that he must venture forth, seeking out other threats to the balance of magic and fulfilling the role bestowed upon him by the Guardian.

With a heavy heart, Jasper bid farewell to Maelis and the villagers, promising to return whenever the need arose. As he departed Almsley, the crystal pendant around his neck pulsed with the power of the mountain, guiding him towards his next adventure.

The world was vast, and the forces of darkness were ever-present, but Jasper Ebonshire was undeterred. With the power of the mystical mountain at his command, he would face whatever challenges lay ahead, defending the realm of magic and ensuring that the shadows would never again threaten the valley he called home.

And so, the tale of Jasper Ebonshire, the young magician chosen by fate, continued. His legend would grow, his deeds recounted in songs and stories that spread across the land. And though he would face countless trials and tribulations, he would never forget the lessons he had learned on that mystical mountain, or the people and the village that had shaped him into the hero he had become.

Screenplay

Title: Mountain Magic

copyright 2023 peacockOriginals.com LLC

FADE IN:

EXT. ALMSLEY VILLAGE - DAY

A peaceful, verdant valley cradles the quaint village of ALMSLEY. Villagers go about their daily routines: tending to livestock, working in the fields, and visiting the bustling marketplace.

INT. MAELIS' HUT - DAY

JASPER EBONSHIRE (18), a young magician with a spark of determination in his eyes, watches as his mentor, the blind witch MAELIS (60s), prepares a potion. Jasper is eager to learn but feels limited by his surroundings.

JASPER:
There must be more to magic than what we have here, Maelis. I want to learn, to grow!

MAELIS:
Patience, Jasper. You have much to learn, but remember: power comes with great responsibility.

EXT. ALMSLEY VILLAGE - DAY

Jasper gazes towards the distant mountains, a determination growing within him. He decides to leave Almsley to seek the mystical mountain.

EXT. MOUNTAIN LANDSCAPE - VARIOUS

Jasper faces various obstacles: crossing a raging river, scaling a steep cliff, and battling a giant WILD BEAST.

EXT. MYSTICAL MOUNTAIN - DAY

At last, Jasper reaches the peak of the mystical mountain. A sense of awe and wonder overcomes him as the mountain's magic hums in the air.

INT. MOUNTAIN SANCTUM - DAY

Jasper enters a hidden chamber, where he meets the GUARDIAN, an ancient being who has protected the mountain's secrets for millennia. The Guardian informs Jasper of his destiny as a protector of the balance of magic.

MONTAGE: JASPER'S TRAINING

The Guardian teaches Jasper powerful spells, harnessing elemental forces, and communing with spirits. Jasper's skills and knowledge grow exponentially.

EXT. MYSTICAL MOUNTAIN - DAY

Jasper, now a powerful magician, descends the mountain, armed with newfound knowledge and a crystal pendant gifted by the Guardian.

EXT. ALMSLEY VILLAGE - DAY

Jasper returns to find Almsley shrouded in darkness. The once-thriving marketplace is abandoned, and the cobblestone streets eerily empty.

INT. MAELIS' HUT - DAY

Jasper discovers a note from Maelis, detailing the threat of the evil sorcerer MORVANE. He learns that she is hiding at the edge of the Whispering Woods.

EXT. WHISPERING WOODS - DAY

Jasper reunites with Maelis, who expresses pride in his growth. Together, they prepare for the upcoming battle against Morvane.

EXT. ALMSLEY VILLAGE SQUARE - DAY

The climactic battle between Jasper, Maelis, and Morvane takes place. Magic crackles in the air, and the forces of light and darkness clash.

EXT. ALMSLEY VILLAGE SQUARE - DAY (AFTERMATH)

Jasper and Maelis emerge victorious, but the village is severely damaged. They know they must work together to restore their home.

MONTAGE: REBUILDING ALMSLEY

Jasper and Maelis work alongside the villagers to rebuild Almsley, restoring it to its former glory. The marketplace bustles with life once more.

EXT. ALMSLEY VILLAGE - DAY

Jasper bids an emotional farewell to Maelis and the villagers, promising to return when needed. He sets off to fulfill his destiny as a protector of the balance of magic.

EXT. ROAD OUT OF ALMSLEY - DAY

As Jasper embarks on his journey, the crystal pendant around his neck pulses with the power of the mystical mountain. He is ready to face new challenges and protect the world of magic.

FADE OUT.

THE END

Shooting Script

Title: Mountain Magic

copyright 2023 peacockOriginals.com LLC

SLUGLINE: EXT. ALMSLEY VILLAGE - DAY

AERIAL SHOT of a peaceful, verdant valley cradling the quaint village of ALMSLEY.

SHOT 1 - WIDE SHOT of villagers going about their daily routines: tending to livestock, working in the fields, and visiting the bustling marketplace.

SLUGLINE: INT. MAELIS' HUT - DAY

SHOT 2 - MEDIUM SHOT of JASPER EBONSHIRE (18) watching his mentor, the blind witch MAELIS (60s), as she prepares a potion.

SHOT 3 - CLOSE-UP of Jasper's face, showing his eagerness to learn.

JASPER:
There must be more to magic than what we have here, Maelis. I want to learn, to grow!

SHOT 4 - MEDIUM SHOT of Maelis, responding to Jasper with a note of caution.

MAELIS:
Patience, Jasper. You have much to learn, but remember: power comes with great responsibility.

SLUGLINE: EXT. ALMSLEY VILLAGE - DAY

SHOT 5 - MEDIUM SHOT of Jasper gazing towards the distant mountains.

SHOT 6 - CLOSE-UP of Jasper's face, filled with determination.

Desert Roadtrip

[in the style of Hunter S. Thompson]

The sun was already a bloodied orb of molten gold, sinking fast into the horizon, when our anti-hero, Lazlo Jenkins, purveyor of ones and zeros and erstwhile Googler, decided that it was high time he escaped the confines of his San Francisco prison. The City by the Bay had become a relentless vise, slowly squeezing the life out of him in a continuous, cacophonous rhythm.

Lazlo was a man of peculiar tastes and habits. He felt suffocated, laid off from the digital kingdom he once ruled, left bereft of purpose and pleasure. In the depths of his despair, he reached out to his ex-girlfriend, a beatnik painter with a penchant for collecting broken hearts and rusted vehicles. She agreed to lend him her extra car – a '67 Chevy Impala, all chrome and character, baptized in peeling burgundy paint. It was a poor excuse for a chariot, but it would do the job.

As Lazlo eased the Impala onto the highway, he left behind a plume of exhaust smoke and the shattered remains of his once-promising career. The plan was simple: a journey into the desert, a pilgrimage into the great American void, a quest for solace in the arms of desolation. The wind ripped at his face, howling like a demented coyote, as the engine roared beneath him, hungry for the open road.

The Mojave stretched out before him, a vast wasteland with a thousand tongues, whispering secrets that only the mad and the damned could understand. Lazlo was both, and he felt the call of the desert as surely as a junkie feels the itch for another hit. He was ready to commune with the spirits of the void, to rip the veil of reality asunder and discover what lay beyond.

His first stop was a lonely bar on the outskirts of Barstow, a forsaken outpost where the damned and the desperate drank away their sorrows, and the bartender had the gaze of a man who'd seen too many sunsets and not enough sunrises. Lazlo sauntered in, his eyes wild with purpose, and took a seat at the bar.

"What'll it be?" the bartender rasped, his voice like sandpaper and sagebrush.

"Give me something to remember and something to forget," Lazlo replied, his eyes gleaming with the desperate fire of a man on the edge.

The bartender nodded and set to work, his hands moving with the slow precision of a desert tortoise. He placed two shots before

Lazlo – one an iridescent blue, the other a murky amber that seemed to swallow the light. Lazlo hesitated for a moment, then downed both, the liquid fire searing a path down his throat.

As the world tilted and swayed, Lazlo stumbled back to the Impala, a crooked grin plastered across his face. The road beckoned once more, and he answered the call, pushing the old Chevy harder, faster, deeper into the unforgiving desert night. The stars above glittered like the eyes of a thousand demons, and the wind laughed as it tore at his hair.

Lazlo's journey took him through the sun-bleached bones of forgotten towns, past rusted gas stations and crumbling diners, into the very heart of the desert. He met strange, twisted denizens along the way – a one-eyed hitchhiker with a voice like a broken violin; a gas station attendant who sold snake oil and salvation in equal measure; a dancer at a roadside honky-tonk whose beauty was only matched by the emptiness in her eyes.

Each encounter left Lazlo changed, a little more broken, a little more lost. But still he pressed on, driven by a mad desire to find solace in the shifting sands and merciless sun. The Impala became an extension of his own twisted soul, a mechanical beast that devoured the miles and belched smoke like the fires of hell.

On the third day, Lazlo found himself in the shadow of a great mesa, its sheer red cliffs looming over him like the walls of an ancient fortress. The air was thick with dust and the ghosts of a thousand nameless wanderers who had come before him, seeking answers in the unforgiving heart of the desert.

A gnarled old man sat in the shade of a twisted Joshua tree, his eyes the color of the sky and his beard a tangled mass of white. Lazlo approached, drawn by an inexplicable magnetism, and the old man raised a gnarled hand in greeting.

"Seek ye solace, wanderer?" the old man croaked, his voice like the whisper of sand against stone.

Lazlo nodded, his eyes wide with wonder and fear. "I seek the truth, old man – the truth of this desert and of my own damned soul."

The old man leaned back against the tree, his eyes twinkling with mirth and madness. "The desert holds many truths, wanderer, but they are not easily won. You must face your own demons, confront the shadows that lurk within your heart."

Lazlo hesitated, then sank to his knees in the dust, his desperation laid bare. "I will do whatever it takes, old man. Show me the way."

The old man's laughter echoed off the cliffs, a sound both chilling and intoxicating. "Very well, then. When the sun sinks below the horizon, you must climb to the top of this mesa. There, you will find your solace – or your doom."

As the sun dipped below the horizon, Lazlo set off, climbing the mesa with a feverish intensity. His hands bled from the effort, his breath came in ragged gasps, but he refused to relent, driven by an irresistible need to uncover the truth that lay waiting for him at the summit.

Finally, after what seemed like an eternity, Lazlo reached the top, his body trembling with exhaustion and anticipation. The stars wheeled overhead, their cold, indifferent gaze fixed upon the lone figure standing at the edge of the abyss.

Lazlo stared into the void, his heart pounding, and waited for the revelation that would set him free – or destroy him utterly.

All night, Lazlo waited, his body shivering with cold and anticipation as the stars wheeled overhead. The darkness around him was oppressive, a physical weight that threatened to crush the breath from his lungs. He felt his sanity begin to fray at the edges, the long, silent hours stretching out before him like an abyss.

As the first faint light of dawn began to creep over the horizon, Lazlo was seized by a sudden, uncontrollable panic. He had waited too long, allowed the night to slip through his fingers like sand. Desperation lent him a new strength, and he began to scramble up the mesa, heedless of the cuts and bruises that tore at his flesh.

Lazlo ran, stumbled, and even crawled, his entire being focused on reaching the top before the sun could rise and steal away the truth he sought. The mesa seemed to grow taller with each passing second, as if the very earth itself was conspiring to keep him from his goal.

His breath came in ragged gasps, and his muscles screamed in protest, but Lazlo refused to relent. He knew that if he failed now, if he allowed the sun to rise before he reached the summit, he would be lost forever, condemned to a life of emptiness and regret.

At last, with the sun's first rays just beginning to break over the horizon, Lazlo reached the top of the mesa. His body was battered and bleeding, but his spirit blazed with a wild, triumphant fire. He had conquered the mountain and, in doing so, conquered himself.

But there was little time to savor his victory. The sun was rising fast, and Lazlo knew that he must act quickly if he was to uncover the truth that awaited him. He cast his gaze around the summit, searching for any sign of the revelation he had been promised.

What Lazlo saw was not the answer he expected or desired, but it was the truth he needed. He found no hidden shrine, no oracle to bestow enlightenment. Instead, he discovered a simple, unremarkable cairn of stones, set against the backdrop of the vast, unforgiving desert.

Lazlo approached the stones, his heart heavy with disappointment and a dawning realization. He had sought solace in the arms of the desert, believing that the truth he needed lay hidden in the sands and the stars. But the desert had given him a different kind of truth – a revelation born of struggle and pain, of fear and loneliness.

As the sun climbed higher in the sky, Lazlo knew that his journey had come to an end. The truth he sought was not out here, amid the dust and the desolation. It was within him, locked away in the darkest recesses of his soul. To find solace, he would need to face his demons and embrace the shadows that lurked within his heart.

And so, with the sun casting its golden light over the mesa and the desert stretching out before him like a promise, Lazlo Jenkins turned and began the long journey home.

Screenplay

Title: Desert Roadtrip

copyright 2023 peacockOriginals.com LLC

INT. LAZLO'S SAN FRANCISCO APARTMENT - DAY

Lazlo, a disheveled San Francisco programmer, paces around his small, cluttered apartment. His eyes are bloodshot, and his hands tremble as he dials a number on his phone.

LAZLO (into phone) Hey... it's me, Lazlo. I need a favor.

EXT. BEATNIK PAINTER'S HOUSE - DAY

Lazlo stands in front of a colorful, eclectic house. His ex-girlfriend, a beatnik painter, hands him the keys to her '67 Chevy Impala.

BEATNIK PAINTER (smiling) Take care of her, Lazlo. And take care of yourself.

Lazlo nods solemnly and walks over to the car.

EXT. HIGHWAY - DAY

Lazlo pushes the Impala onto the open highway, leaving San Francisco behind.

EXT. BAR OUTSKIRTS OF BARSTOW - NIGHT

Lazlo enters the lonely bar, taking a seat. The BARTENDER approaches.

BARTENDER What'll it be?

LAZLO Give me something to remember and something to forget.

The bartender pours two shots. Lazlo downs both, then stumbles back to the Impala.

EXT. MOJAVE DESERT - VARIOUS LOCATIONS - DAY/NIGHT

Montage of Lazlo's journey through the desert, meeting the ONE-EYED HITCHHIKER, the SNAKE OIL SALESMAN, and the DANCER.

EXT. MESA - DAY

Lazlo encounters the GNARLED OLD MAN under a Joshua tree.

GNARLED OLD MAN Seek ye solace, wanderer?

LAZLO I seek the truth, old man - the truth of this desert and of my own damned soul.

GNARLED OLD MAN When the sun sinks below the horizon, you must climb to the top of this mesa. There, you will find your solace - or your doom.

EXT. MESA - NIGHT

Lazlo waits at the base of the mesa as night falls.

EXT. MESA - DAWN

Driven by panic, Lazlo races to the top of the mesa, climbing with desperation.

EXT. MESA SUMMIT - DAWN

Lazlo reaches the summit just before the sun rises. He discovers the cairn of stones and realizes the truth he sought was within himself all along.

EXT. MESA SUMMIT - DAY

Lazlo stands at the edge of the summit, taking in the vast desert landscape. With newfound determination, he begins his descent and starts his journey home.

FADE OUT.

THE END

Shooting Script

Title: Desert Roadtrip

copyright 2023 peacockOriginals.com LLC

INT. LAZLO'S SAN FRANCISCO APARTMENT - DAY

Lazlo paces around his small, cluttered apartment, visibly distressed. He picks up his phone, hesitates, then dials a number.

INSERT: PHONE SCREEN showing "Ex-Girlfriend"

LAZLO Hey... it's me, Lazlo. I need a favor.

EXT. BEATNIK PAINTER'S HOUSE - DAY

Lazlo stands in front of a colorful, eclectic house. His ex-girlfriend, a beatnik painter, hands him the keys to her '67 Chevy Impala. They exchange a few words, and Lazlo walks over to the car.

EXT. HIGHWAY - DAY

Lazlo drives the Impala onto the open highway, leaving San Francisco behind.

EXT. BAR OUTSKIRTS OF BARSTOW - NIGHT

Lazlo enters the lonely bar, taking a seat. The BARTENDER approaches. They exchange a few words, and the bartender pours two shots. Lazlo downs both and stumbles back to the Impala.

EXT. MOJAVE DESERT - VARIOUS LOCATIONS - DAY/NIGHT

Montage of Lazlo's journey through the desert, meeting the ONE-EYED HITCHHIKER, the SNAKE OIL SALESMAN, and the DANCER.

EXT. MESA - DAY

Lazlo encounters the GNARLED OLD MAN under a Joshua tree. They exchange a few words, and the old man gives Lazlo cryptic instructions.

EXT. MESA - NIGHT

Lazlo waits at the base of the mesa as night falls.

EXT. MESA - DAWN

Driven by panic, Lazlo races to the top of the mesa, climbing with desperation.

EXT. MESA SUMMIT - DAWN

Lazlo reaches the summit just before the sun rises. He discovers the cairn of stones and has a moment of realization.

EXT. MESA SUMMIT - DAY

Lazlo stands at the edge of the summit, taking in the vast desert landscape. With newfound determination, he begins his descent and starts his journey home.

FADE OUT.

THE END

Escape from Chicago

[in the style of Willa Cather]

Under a heavy Chicago sky, the midnight train waited to depart, releasing clouds of smoke from its hulking black engine, like some ancient dragon ready to spread its wings. On the platform, the gas lamps cast an eerie glow upon the passengers milling about, their voices hushed and expectant. Among them, a young girl, no more than sixteen, stood with her back pressed against the rough brick wall. Her eyes, wide with fear and anticipation, darted from one face to another as she clutched a small worn satchel to her chest.

The girl's name was Alice, and she had suffered torments she dared not remember. Her past life seemed now like a terrible fever dream, and she was resolved to put as much distance between herself and her abuser as possible. The train that lay before her, she imagined, was her escape from the prison of her existence.

As Alice boarded the train, she felt a sudden weightlessness. The air seemed fresher, and the world outside the window seemed brighter, even though the night was dark and full of shadows. With each mile that passed, she felt the chains of her past loosen and fall away. For the first time in her young life, she believed that she might find freedom.

In her journey, Alice encountered an array of strangers, each with their own stories, each seeking their own escape. There was Mrs. Evers, a widow with a brood of unruly children, who smiled kindly at Alice and offered her a seat in their boisterous compartment. Alice's heart warmed as she observed the widow's patience and love for her children, even in the face of exhaustion and despair.

Then, there was the enigmatic Mr. Thorne, a tall man with a polished air and a rakish smile. He tipped his hat to Alice and offered to share a meal with her in the dining car. Alice was initially taken by his charm, but as the miles rolled on, she noticed a predatory glint in his eyes. When he mentioned the money that could be made in the saloons and dance halls of the west, Alice felt a cold shiver run down her spine.

And there was Phoebe, a quiet woman with a face marked by sorrow, who spent hours staring out the window at the passing landscape. She told Alice of her dreams of becoming a schoolteacher in a small prairie town, of finding solace in the wide-open spaces and the kindness of strangers. Her voice was like a soothing balm, and her gentle words wove themselves around Alice's bruised heart.

As the train rumbled on, Alice felt her life unfolding before her like the tracks stretching out to the horizon. She had come to know the kindness of strangers, and also the danger that lurked beneath the surface of their smiles. In the ever-changing landscape outside her window, she began to glimpse the possibility of a new life.

The train stopped at a dusty little station, and Phoebe stepped out into the warm evening air. She turned to Alice, her eyes full of hope and sadness. "You must choose your path, Alice," she said softly. "Do not let your history define you. Remember, the world is wide, and there are good people out there. Trust your heart, and it will guide you."

Alice watched as Phoebe disappeared into the twilight, her heart swelling with gratitude and longing. As the train pulled away from the platform, she knew that her journey had only just begun. The world was vast and full of possibilities, and she was determined to find her place in it.

As the train rolled on, the night gave way to a sun-bleached dawn, washing the world in shades of gold and pink. Alice watched the landscape shift, from the vast plains to the rolling hills, and felt her heart swell with each passing mile. The train became a sanctuary for her, a moving vessel carrying her from the darkness of her earlier life into the uncertain light of her future.

One evening, as the sun dipped below the horizon, Alice found herself alone in the observation car. The world outside the window had become a dark tapestry, woven with the threads of possibility. Her thoughts turned to Phoebe, who had seemed like a beacon of hope in an otherwise uncertain world. Alice wondered if she would ever find the courage to reach for her own dreams.

As the train glided through the night, a young man entered the observation car. He was tall, with broad shoulders and a mop of curly hair that fell into his eyes. His face was weathered, as if he had spent years under the sun, and yet there was a kindness in his gaze that Alice found comforting.

"I'm Benjamin," he said, extending a hand towards Alice. She hesitated for a moment, then accepted it, feeling the warmth of his calloused fingers against her skin. They spoke for hours, their voices low and intimate, as the world outside raced by. Benjamin told Alice of his plans to start a small ranch, of his desire to work the land and live a simple, honest life.

Alice's heart began to race, her thoughts filled with visions of wide-open spaces and a life free from the specter of before. She imagined herself working alongside Benjamin, their days filled with hard work and laughter, their evenings spent beneath a canopy of stars. It was a life she had never dared to dream of, and yet, in that moment, it felt as if it were within her reach.

Days passed, and as the train drew closer to its final destination, Alice found herself torn between the excitement of the unknown and the fear of stepping off the train and into the world beyond. She had come to see the train as a cocoon, a haven that protected her from the harsh realities that awaited her. And yet, she knew that she could not stay on the train forever.

On the morning of the final day, Alice awoke to find a small bundle at the foot of her seat. It was wrapped in brown paper and tied with a simple string. Benjamin stood nearby, his eyes shining with anticipation. "I thought you might like this," he said, his voice filled with a quiet hope. "Something to remember the journey by."

Alice unwrapped the package to find a small journal, its cover embossed with a delicate pattern of flowers and leaves. Tears filled her eyes as she realized the significance of the gift – a chance to write her own story, to create a new life unburdened by the weight of her memories.

As the train pulled into the station, Alice clutched the journal to her chest, her heart pounding with a mixture of fear and excitement. The world beyond the train was vast and unknown, but she knew that she must step forward and embrace it, or risk being forever defined by a darkness. With a deep breath, she stepped onto the platform, her eyes filled with the bright promise of a new beginning.

With her newfound sense of freedom, Alice decided to settle in the bustling town that the train had carried her to. Despite its quaint appearance, the town was alive with the hum of travelers and locals alike. Searching for a way to earn a living, Alice soon found work in a local café situated near the train station. The café, called "The Whistle Stop," was a popular spot for train passengers and townsfolk, and Alice quickly became a familiar face to the regulars. Her days were filled with the aroma of freshly brewed coffee and the bustle of hungry patrons, and she found a sense of purpose and camaraderie among her fellow workers.

It was in this small café that Alice met James, a ruggedly handsome farm worker hailing from Canada. His sun-kissed skin and broad shoulders bore the marks of his labor, but it was his easy smile and warm eyes that drew Alice to him. James had been traveling through the area, working on various farms and ranches, when he stumbled upon "The Whistle Stop" one fateful afternoon.

Over steaming cups of coffee, they shared stories of their lives, dreams, and the places they had left behind. As the days went by, their conversations grew deeper, and Alice found herself looking forward to every moment she spent in James's company. In him, she saw a kindred spirit, someone who, like her, was searching for a sense of belonging and a place to call home.

As the seasons changed and the days grew shorter, Alice found herself falling for James. She couldn't help but imagine a life with him, working side by side on a sprawling farm beneath the vast, open skies of the Canadian prairie. Her heart ached with longing, but she hesitated, held back by the fear of the unknown.

One evening, as the sun dipped below the horizon, painting the sky with a brilliant tapestry of color, Alice found herself standing at the edge of the train tracks, clutching her worn satchel to her chest. She thought of Benjamin and the journal he had given her, its pages now filled with her dreams and heartaches. She thought of Phoebe and her words of wisdom, urging her to trust her heart and choose her own path.

As Alice stood there, torn between the life she had built in the town and the uncertain future that lay before her, she heard the distant whistle of an approaching train. It sounded like a call to adventure, beckoning her to step onto the tracks and follow her heart, wherever it may lead.

With a deep breath, Alice turned back towards the café, her heart pounding with a mixture of fear and excitement. Inside, James was waiting, his warm eyes filled with the promise of a new beginning. As she reached out and took his calloused hand in hers, Alice knew that she had found her place in the world, and that together, they would write the next chapter of their story.

Alice and James continued to grow closer, their love blossoming like the flowers that sprung up around the town as winter melted away. They spent their days exploring the countryside and their evenings lost in conversation, sharing their deepest hopes and fears. With each passing day, Alice felt the shadows of her past recede further into the distance, replaced by the warm glow of the life she was building with James.

However, one fateful day, as they sat beside a gently babbling creek, James's face grew somber, and his eyes seemed to cloud with an unspoken burden. Sensing his unease, Alice reached out and took his hand, encouraging him to share what was weighing on his mind.

With a heavy sigh, James revealed a secret that he had been carrying ever since he first arrived in town: he was on the run from the law in Canada. He had been falsely accused of a crime he did not commit, and rather than face the prospect of imprisonment for a misdeed he did not commit, he had chosen to flee, leaving his old life and family behind.

As James's words tumbled out, Alice's heart grew heavy with the weight of this new knowledge. The man she had come to love was not only a fugitive, but also a man tormented by the loss of his home and family. She saw the pain in his eyes, and it reminded her of her own past, of the darkness she had left behind and the fear that had haunted her every step.

In that moment, Alice knew that she could not turn away from James. She had learned from her own journey that everyone deserved a second chance, a chance to find redemption and happiness in spite of the darkness that threatened to consume them. She looked into James's eyes, filled with a mixture of fear and hope, and made a decision that would alter the course of their lives forever.

Together, they would return to Canada, to face the demons of James's and clear his name. They knew that the journey would be fraught with danger and uncertainty, but they also knew that their love was strong enough to weather any storm that came their way.

As they prepared to leave the life they had built in the small town, Alice felt the familiar stirrings of fear and doubt, the echoes of her past that still lingered in the corners of her heart. But she also felt something else, something she had never experienced before: a sense of purpose and determination, born from the love she shared with James.

Hand in hand, they boarded a train bound for the north, leaving behind the safety of the town and the memories of the life they had built there. As the train pulled away from the station, Alice clutched her worn satchel to her chest, her heart pounding with the knowledge that she was embarking on a new adventure, one that would test the limits of her strength and the depth of her love.

But as the miles rolled by and the landscape outside their window shifted once more, Alice knew that they would face whatever challenges lay ahead, together. They would write their own story, carving a new path through the unknown and fighting for the life and love they so desperately sought. And in doing so, they would find the redemption and freedom that had eluded them for so long.

Screenplay

Title: Escape from Chicago

copyright 2023 peacockOriginals.com LLC

INT. THE WHISTLE STOP CAFE - DAY

Alice, a young woman with a kind but haunted face, works at the counter of the bustling cafe, pouring coffee and serving food to a mixture of travelers and townsfolk.

EXT. THE WHISTLE STOP CAFE - DAY

James, a ruggedly handsome farm worker, approaches the cafe. He hesitates for a moment before entering.

INT. THE WHISTLE STOP CAFE - DAY

Alice notices James and smiles as she approaches his table.

ALICE What can I get for you today?

JAMES Just a cup of coffee, please.

Alice pours him a cup of coffee and joins him at his table. They talk and laugh, quickly growing closer.

EXT. COUNTRYSIDE - DAY

Alice and James walk together, hand in hand, through fields of tall grass. They share their stories, dreams, and fears.

EXT. CREEK - DAY

James, looking somber, sits beside Alice on the grassy bank of a gently babbling creek.

JAMES Alice, there's something I need to tell you.

ALICE (taking his hand) What is it, James?

JAMES I'm on the run from the law in Canada. I was falsely accused, and I had to leave my family and home behind.

Alice listens, her heart aching for James and the pain he carries.

ALICE We'll face this together. Let's go back to Canada and clear your name.

INT. TRAIN STATION - DAY

Alice and James stand on the platform, holding hands, as they prepare to board a train to Canada. Alice clutches her worn satchel to her chest, her eyes filled with determination.

EXT. TRAIN - DAY

The train departs from the station, carrying Alice and James on their journey to face the past and fight for their future.

FADE OUT.

Shooting Script

Title: Escape from Chicago

copyright 2023 peacockOriginals.com LLC

INT. THE WHISTLE STOP CAFE - DAY

Camera pans across the busy cafe, filled with CUSTOMERS and the sound of chatter. Focus on ALICE as she moves from table to table, taking orders and serving food.

EXT. THE WHISTLE STOP CAFE - DAY

JAMES approaches the cafe entrance, pausing for a moment before entering.

INT. THE WHISTLE STOP CAFE - DAY

ALICE notices JAMES, smiles warmly, and walks over to his table.

ANGLE ON ALICE:

ALICE What can I get for you today?

ANGLE ON JAMES:

JAMES Just a cup of coffee, please.

ALICE pours coffee for JAMES, then takes a seat at his table. Camera pulls back to reveal them laughing and talking as they grow closer.

EXT. COUNTRYSIDE - DAY

ALICE and JAMES walk hand in hand through fields of tall grass, talking and laughing.

EXT. CREEK - DAY

JAMES, looking somber, sits beside ALICE on the grassy bank of a babbling creek.

ANGLE ON JAMES:

JAMES Alice, there's something I need to tell you.

ANGLE ON ALICE:

ALICE (taking his hand) What is it, James?

ANGLE ON JAMES:

JAMES I'm on the run from the law in Canada. I was falsely accused, and I had to leave my family and home behind.

CLOSE-UP on ALICE's face, showing her empathy and determination.

ALICE We'll face this together. Let's go back to Canada and clear your name.

INT. TRAIN STATION - DAY

ALICE and JAMES stand on the platform, holding hands, as they prepare to board a train to Canada. ALICE clutches her worn satchel to her chest.

ANGLE ON ALICE AND JAMES:

They share a determined look, ready to face the challenges ahead.

EXT. TRAIN - DAY

The train departs from the station. Camera pulls back, revealing the landscape as ALICE and JAMES embark on their journey to confront the past and fight for their future.

FADE OUT.

Cast Away

[in the style of Anne Rice]

On the cusp of twilight, when the sun's last dying rays bled scarlet and gold into the ever-expanding canvas of the sky, he washed ashore. The waves, having toyed with him for the better part of the day, relinquished their hold at last, leaving him sprawled like some divine offering upon the beach. Half-naked, his body bore the telltale marks of the sea's violent caress; salt-caked hair, sunburnt skin, and the ocean's brine embedded within every crevice of his being.

Our tale begins thus, in the solace of the forsaken island, where the distant cries of gulls and the whispers of the wind were the only witnesses to his arrival. What misfortune had led him to this desolate stretch of land, a realm untouched by the hands of civilization? What calamities had conspired to render him so wretched and lost?

The man, for his part, stirred only when the last vestiges of daylight had all but vanished, surrendering to the inexorable embrace of night. He awoke to the rhythmic lullaby of the waves, his ears attuned to the ceaseless susurration that was the island's dirge. Slowly, painfully, he rose from his prone position, propping himself up on trembling arms. His eyes, heavy with the weight of an unknown past, surveyed the land before him.

As the night unfurled its ebony cloak, he found himself bathed in the silvery light of the full moon, which cast its cold, unfeeling gaze upon his vulnerable form. A bitter wind, laden with the scent of brine and the mysteries of the sea, skated across his exposed flesh, raising goosebumps in its wake. With a gasp, he rose to his feet, swaying precariously as he struggled to maintain his balance.

An island, he realized with a dull sense of dread, was all that stood between him and the endless expanse of the ocean. It stretched before him, a vast and desolate landscape carved from the unforgiving hand of nature. There was a sinister beauty to it, a haunting allure that beckoned him with promises of redemption and salvation.

Yet, in the depths of his heart, he knew that this place was a sepulcher, a tomb for the forgotten and the damned. It was a land forsaken by both gods and men, a realm of eternal solitude where the ghosts of the past roamed free, condemned to wander the earth in search of absolution. As the wind howled its mournful dirge, he found himself drawn to the heart of the island, towards the bowels of the abyss that awaited him.

He walked for what seemed like an eternity, his feet sinking into the soft, damp sand with each heavy step. The world around him was a cacophony of shadows and whispers, the darkness punctuated by the erratic dance of fireflies and the eerie glow of phosphorescent fungi. The air was thick with the scent of decay and the promise of death, a miasma that clung to his skin like a shroud.

As he ventured deeper into the island, the landscape began to change. The beach, with its gentle undulations, gave way to a terrain marked by jagged rocks and gnarled roots that seemed to claw at his feet, as if the very earth sought to hold him fast. He traversed this treacherous ground with a dogged determination, driven by a force he could not name or comprehend.

It was in the heart of this primeval forest that he stumbled upon her. She lay there, a vision of ethereal beauty, her silken hair fanned out around her like a halo.

Her alabaster skin seemed to shimmer beneath the moonlight, a stark contrast to the darkness that surrounded her. She appeared to be sleeping, her slender form swathed in a gown of gossamer threads that clung to her body like a lover's embrace. Her face, a portrait of serenity, was framed by delicate curls that cascaded down her shoulders like rivulets of ink.

Drawn to her by a power he could not resist, he found himself kneeling at her side, his fingers hovering inches from her cold flesh. He hesitated, his heart pounding in his chest, a mixture of awe and trepidation coursing through his veins. With a trembling hand, he reached out to touch her, the briefest brush of her skin sending shivers down his spine.

She stirred, her eyelids fluttering open to reveal eyes the color of a storm-tossed sea, gray and tempestuous, filled with the promise of both salvation and damnation. Her gaze held him captive, ensnaring him in a web of desire and longing that he could neither deny nor escape. In that instant, he knew that she was his destiny, his reason for being stranded upon this forsaken island.

"Who are you?" he whispered, his voice barely audible above the wind's mournful cry.

"I am the one you seek," she replied, her voice a melody that tugged at his heartstrings, filling him with a sense of yearning that he had never known. "I am the one who will show you the way, the path to redemption and absolution."

He frowned, unable to comprehend her words. "I do not understand," he said. "What is it that you offer me?"

She smiled, her lips curving into a crescent that seemed to rival the moon itself. "I offer you the chance to atone for your sins, to reclaim the life that was stolen from you. I am the key to your salvation, the means by which you will find your way home."

He stared at her, his mind racing as he struggled to make sense of her enigmatic words. A part of him, a part that he could not silence, yearned to believe her, to trust in the possibility of redemption. But another part, a part buried deep within the recesses of his soul, warned him against such folly, urged him to turn away from this siren and her alluring promises.

"Can you truly help me?" he asked, his voice laden with doubt and uncertainty.

She reached out, her fingers brushing against his cheek in a gesture that was both tender and seductive. "I can," she whispered, her breath hot against his skin. "But first, you must help me."

His eyes widened, his heart quickening in his chest. "What do you need?" he inquired, willing to offer her anything and everything in exchange for the salvation she promised.

"Release me," she murmured, her gaze never leaving his. "Free me from this prison, and I will show you the way home."

He hesitated, his instincts warning him against such folly. But in the end, his desire for redemption won out, drowning out the voice of reason that whispered in the back of his mind. With a nod, he agreed to her terms, sealing his fate and binding their destinies together.

Thus began their journey, a tale of love and betrayal, of hope and despair, that would span the length and breadth of the island. Together, they would navigate the treacherous terrain, their souls entwined, their hearts bound by the promise of salvation. But as the days stretched into weeks, and the weeks into months, he would come to realize that the path to redemption was fraught with danger and deceit and that the price of salvation might be far greater than he had ever imagined.

As they journeyed deeper into the heart of the island, the landscape transformed into a twisted, nightmarish world, where the very fabric of reality seemed to warp and fray. The trees grew tall and gnarled, their branches twisted into grotesque shapes that seemed to leer at them as they passed. The air was thick with a miasma of decay, a putrid scent that clung to their clothes and hair, a constant reminder of the darkness that surrounded them.

The woman, who called herself Isolde, led him through this desolate land with a determination that bordered on obsession. She seemed to know the island's secrets, guiding him through hidden passageways and treacherous paths that only she could see. Her eyes, once a storm-tossed gray, had turned black as coal, their depths filled with a hunger that he could not name.

As the days passed, he began to notice a change in her demeanor. The woman who had once been a vision of ethereal beauty had become gaunt and hollow, her once-radiant skin stretched tight across her bones. Her eyes, once filled with the promise of salvation, now burned with a feverish intensity, their depths filled with shadows that seemed to dance and flicker like the flames of a dying fire.

He tried to ignore the warning signs, the whispered doubts that plagued his thoughts and haunted his dreams. But as they ventured further into the abyss, he could not deny the truth that gnawed at his soul: that the woman he had sworn to save was, in fact, the very darkness that threatened to consume them both.

As they neared the heart of the island, they stumbled upon a hidden chamber, a subterranean cavern that pulsed with an ancient, malevolent power. The walls were adorned with strange, twisted symbols, the remnants of a forgotten language that seemed to writhe and twist before his very eyes. And at the center of it all, a churning vortex of darkness, an abyss so black and vast that it threatened to swallow them whole.

It was here that Isolde revealed her true purpose, the reason for her desperate quest for salvation. She had been imprisoned on the island by an ancient, vengeful deity, a being of unimaginable power and cruelty that had sought to claim her as its own. She had resisted, her spirit bound within the heart of the island, her body cast upon the shore as a broken, lifeless shell.

The only way to break the curse, to free her spirit and reclaim her body, was to sacrifice another in her place, to offer up a soul to the deity in exchange for her own. And so she had lured him to the island, bound him to her with promises of redemption and salvation, all in the hopes of claiming his life as her own.

Faced with this terrible truth, he was forced to make a choice: to offer up his soul in exchange for hers, or to turn his back on the woman he had come to love and leave her to her fate. It was a decision that would haunt him for the rest of his days, a choice that would forever bind him to the forsaken island and the darkness that dwelled within its heart.

In the end, he chose to sacrifice himself, to offer up his soul in exchange for hers. As the vortex swallowed him whole, he felt a strange sense of peace, a quiet acceptance of the fate that awaited him. And as the darkness closed in, he knew that he had made the right choice, that he had given her the gift of life and, in doing so, had found his own redemption.

But as the years passed, and the island grew ever more isolated and desolate, he began to question the wisdom of his decision. His soul, trapped within the heart of the island, was tormented by the whispers of the past and the shadows of the future. He watched as Isolde, now free from her curse, ventured back into the world of men, her once-ethereal beauty restored and her heart filled with a newfound sense of purpose.

Yet, for all her newfound freedom, she did not forget the man who had sacrificed himself for her. She returned to the island, year after year, her visits a balm to his weary soul. She would sit upon the shore, her eyes cast out to sea, and she would tell him stories of the world beyond, of the wonders and horrors that awaited beyond the island's shores.

And as the decades stretched into centuries, and the world beyond the island grew ever more distant and strange, he began to realize that his sacrifice had not been in vain. He had given Isolde the gift of life, and in doing so, had found a measure of redemption in her love and gratitude.

The island, once a forsaken land of darkness and despair, had become a sanctuary, a haven where the ghosts of the past could find solace and peace. And as the years passed, and the world beyond continued to change and evolve, he knew that he had found his true home, a place where he could find solace and redemption in the love of the woman he had saved.

In time, the island's legend grew, whispered tales of a cursed land where a brave castaway had sacrificed himself for the love of a woman, and the ghosts of the past roamed free. Sailors spoke of it in hushed tones, a place of mystery and magic that existed at the edge of the known world.

And as the centuries passed, and the world continued to turn, the island became a beacon, a guiding light that drew the lost and the forsaken to its shores. For they knew that within its heart, they would find the redemption and the absolution that they sought, and that in the love of the woman who had been saved, they would find a measure of peace and solace that they had never known.

Thus ends our tale, a story of love and sacrifice, of hope and despair, that began on a forsaken island at the edge of the world. It is a story that transcends time and space, a testament to the enduring power of love and the indomitable spirit of the human soul. And as the world continues to change and evolve, it is a tale that will be told and retold, a reminder of the power of redemption and the eternal nature of the human heart.

Screenplay

Title: Cast Away

copyright 2023 peacockOriginals.com LLC

EXT. BEACH - TWILIGHT

A castaway, JOHN, half-naked and battered, washes ashore on a deserted island. The last rays of sunlight fade, giving way to the full moon.

INT. JOHN'S MIND - NIGHT

John awakens to the sound of waves, disoriented and frightened. He rises and surveys his surroundings.

EXT. BEACH - NIGHT

John walks deeper into the island, guided by an unknown force. He comes across a sleeping woman, ISOLDE, who appears ethereal and mysterious.

JOHN:
Who are you?

ISOLDE:
I am the one you seek. I am the one who will show you the way, the path to redemption and absolution.

John agrees to help Isolde, and they begin their journey through the island.

EXT. FOREST - DAY

The island's landscape becomes increasingly twisted and nightmarish. Isolde's demeanor changes as well, becoming gaunt and hollow. John starts to doubt her.

EXT. HIDDEN CHAMBER - DAY

Isolde reveals the truth: she lured John to the island to sacrifice his soul to an ancient deity in exchange for her freedom.

John, faced with the choice between his soul and Isolde's, chooses to sacrifice himself.

INT. JOHN'S SOUL - DAY

John's soul is now trapped within the island. He watches as Isolde returns to the world, her beauty and freedom restored.

Isolde visits the island yearly, providing comfort and stories to John's trapped soul.

EXT. BEACH - DAY (CENTURIES LATER)

The island's legend has grown, and the once forsaken land has become a sanctuary for the lost and forsaken.

FADE OUT.

EXT. BEACH - DAY (CENTURIES LATER)

A storm-tossed ship approaches the island, its sails tattered and crew exhausted. Among them, a young woman, LILA, yearns for redemption.

EXT. BEACH - DAY

Lila washes ashore, much like John centuries before. She stumbles upon the same ethereal woman, ISOLDE, who now acts as the island's guardian.

LILA:
Who are you?

ISOLDE:
I am Isolde, the guardian of this island, and the one who will guide you to redemption and peace.

Isolde explains the island's history, John's sacrifice, and how the forsaken now find solace on these shores.

Lila, touched by the tale, decides to stay on the island to find her own redemption.

EXT. ISLAND - VARIOUS SCENES - DAY

Isolde guides Lila through the island's wonders and mysteries, showing her the beauty hidden within its depths.

INT. HIDDEN CHAMBER - DAY

Isolde takes Lila to the hidden chamber where John's soul remains trapped.

LILA:
How can we free him?

ISOLDE:
Only by finding another soul willing to sacrifice itself for him.

Lila contemplates her decision, realizing her own redemption could come from such a sacrifice.

EXT. HIDDEN CHAMBER - DAY

Lila decides to offer her soul in exchange for John's, despite never having met him. Her selfless act frees John's soul, and her own redemption is secured.

INT. JOHN'S SOUL - DAY

John's soul is finally free, and he is reunited with Isolde. The love that transcends time and space blossoms between them.

EXT. BEACH - DAY

The island continues to serve as a sanctuary for the lost and forsaken, a testament to the power of love and redemption.

FADE OUT. THE END

Shooting Script

Title: Cast Away

copyright 2023 peacockOriginals.com LLC

EXT. BEACH - TWILIGHT

A castaway, JOHN, half-naked and battered, washes ashore on a deserted island. The last rays of sunlight fade, giving way to the full moon.

INSERT: John's POV - He opens his eyes and hears the SOUND of waves crashing. He's disoriented and frightened.

EXT. BEACH - NIGHT

John rises and surveys his surroundings. He walks deeper into the island, guided by an unknown force. He comes across a sleeping woman, ISOLDE, who appears ethereal and mysterious.

CLOSE UP: John's face, a mix of curiosity and awe.

JOHN (whispering) Who are you?

ISOLDE (slowly waking up) I am the one you seek. I am the one who will show you the way, the path to redemption and absolution.

John agrees to help Isolde, and they begin their journey through the island.

EXT. FOREST - DAY

The island's landscape becomes increasingly twisted and nightmarish. Isolde's demeanor changes as well, becoming gaunt and hollow. John starts to doubt her.

EXT. HIDDEN CHAMBER - DAY

Isolde reveals the truth: she lured John to the island to sacrifice his soul to an ancient deity in exchange for her freedom.

John, faced with the choice between his soul and Isolde's, chooses to sacrifice himself.

INT. JOHN'S SOUL - DAY

John's soul is now trapped within the island. He watches as Isolde returns to the world, her beauty and freedom restored.

Isolde visits the island yearly, providing comfort and stories to John's trapped soul.

EXT. BEACH - DAY (CENTURIES LATER)

The island's legend has grown, and the once forsaken land has become a sanctuary for the lost and forsaken. A storm-tossed ship approaches the island, its sails tattered and crew exhausted. Among them, a young woman, LILA, yearns for redemption.

EXT. BEACH - DAY

Lila washes ashore, much like John centuries before. She stumbles upon the same ethereal woman, ISOLDE, who now acts as the island's guardian.

LILA Who are you?

ISOLDE I am Isolde, the guardian of this island, and the one who will guide you to redemption and peace.

Isolde explains the island's history, John's sacrifice, and how the forsaken now find solace on these shores. Lila, touched by the tale, decides to stay on the island to find her own redemption.

EXT. ISLAND - VARIOUS SCENES - DAY

Isolde guides Lila through the island's wonders and mysteries, showing her the beauty hidden within its depths.

INT. HIDDEN CHAMBER - DAY

Isolde takes Lila to the hidden chamber where John's soul remains trapped.

LILA How can we free him?

ISOLDE Only by finding another soul willing to sacrifice itself for him.

Lila contemplates her decision, realizing her own redemption could come from such a sacrifice.

EXT. HIDDEN CHAMBER - DAY

Lila decides to offer her soul in exchange for John's, despite never having met him. Her selfless act frees John's soul, and her own redemption is secured.

INT. JOHN'S SOUL - DAY

John's soul is finally free, and he is reunited with Isolde. The love that transcends time and space blossoms between them.

EXT. BEACH - DAY

The island continues to serve as a sanctuary for the lost and forsaken, a testament to the power of love and redemption

FADE IN:

EXT. BEACH - DAY

Isolde and John, hand in hand, walk along the shore. Lila, her soul now part of the island, watches over them, a serene smile on her face.

EXT. ISLAND - VARIOUS SCENES - DAY

Isolde and John explore the island together, rediscovering its beauty and mystery. They tend to the lost and forsaken souls who continue to find refuge on the island, helping them find peace and redemption.

EXT. HIDDEN CHAMBER - DAY

Together, John and Isolde seal the hidden chamber, ensuring that the dark power within can no longer ensnare any more souls.

EXT. BEACH - SUNSET

John and Isolde stand on the beach, gazing out at the horizon as the sun sets, casting brilliant hues of orange and red across the sky. Lila, now the island's new guardian, watches over them from a distance.

JOHN (whispering) Thank you.

ISOLDE (smiling) It was our love that transcended time and space. Our story will continue to inspire others and serve as a reminder of the power of redemption.

As the sun dips below the horizon, Isolde and John embrace, their love eternal and unbreakable, a beacon of hope for all who find refuge on the island.

EXT. ISLAND - NIGHT

The island, now a sanctuary for the lost and forsaken, shines under the moonlight. The souls of those who have found redemption on its shores roam freely, their hearts filled with hope and solace.

FADE OUT:

THE END

The River's Gamble

[in the style of Mark Twain]

In the grand days of the Mississippi River, when steamboats traversed its waters as the floating palaces of fortune and adventure, there lived a man by the name of Jebidiah McAllister. Now, Jebidiah was known far and wide as a poker player of exceptional talent, yet plagued by a luck that could turn sour as a green persimmon.

It was late one summer evening when Jebidiah found himself aboard the magnificent riverboat, The Queen's Vengeance, in a game of poker with gentlemen who were more wolfish than gentlemanly. Luck had been riding him high that night, and he was feeling the touch of the fickle finger of fortune. The night wore on, the game grew thicker, and the stakes grew higher.

As the sun began to rise, Jebidiah's luck took a turn for the worse. He felt a cold shiver run down his spine, a sure sign of impending doom, but in his gambler's heart, he couldn't resist the siren's call of one last hand. He pushed his entire fortune into the center of the table, his hands trembling ever so slightly, and his gaze never leaving the faces of his opponents.

The cards were dealt, and a silence, as heavy as the morning fog, filled the room. Jebidiah's hand was abysmal, a fact which he concealed beneath a mask of perfect calm. With his heart pounding in his chest, he awaited the turn of each card, praying for the providence that would save him from ruin.

As the final card was revealed, a collective gasp rose from the table. Jebidiah's fortune had slipped through his fingers like the muddy waters of the Mississippi itself. The victor, a gentleman of questionable character known as Diamond Jack, claimed his spoils with a grin that would make a weasel jealous.

Left with nary a red cent to his name, Jebidiah had no choice but to work off his debts aboard The Queen's Vengeance as a deckhand. The work was hard and dirty, but he took to it with the fervor of a man determined to regain his fortune and his place among the riverboat elite.

Jebidiah's days were spent mending ropes, scrubbing decks, and hauling cargo, while his nights were filled with dreams of poker tables piled high with riches. Though the callouses on his hands grew thick, his mind remained sharp, honing his skill for the day he would challenge Diamond Jack once more.

One day, as Jebidiah was taking a moment's rest on the deck, his gaze fell upon the stern of the boat, where the name "The Queen's Vengeance" was emblazoned in ornate gold letters. It seemed to him that the name took on a new meaning, as if the boat itself was taking revenge upon him for his foolhardy gamble.

In the months that followed, Jebidiah's reputation grew among the crew as a man of hard work and determination, earning their respect and admiration. The riverboat's captain, a grizzled old sea dog by the name of Horatio Bartholomew, took a particular liking to Jebidiah, seeing in him a spark of the same fire that had driven Horatio to the life of the river.

Captain Bartholomew took Jebidiah under his wing, teaching him the ways of the river, its hidden dangers and bountiful rewards. He spoke of the time when he, too, had been a young man with dreams of fortune and adventure, and how the river had been both his savior and his tormentor.

In the quiet moments between labor and sleep, Jebidiah would find himself reflecting on his past life as a poker player, wondering if perhaps there was more to life than the fickle whims of Lady Luck. As he learned the ways of the river, he felt a growing kinship with the mighty Mississippi, the ever-changing currents echoing the ebb and flow of his own fortunes.

One evening, as Jebidiah stood on the deck, the fiery hues of the setting sun reflecting off the water, a plan began to form in his mind. He would not only work to pay off his debts, but also save every extra penny he could muster, and when the time was right, he would face Diamond Jack once more – not as a desperate gambler, but as a man tempered by adversity and shaped by the river.

As the months turned to years, Jebidiah became a fixture aboard The Queen's Vengeance. The once-renowned poker player had transformed into a skilled riverman, as adept at navigating the treacherous waters as he was at reading the faces of his opponents. Yet in the back of his mind, the memory of that fateful poker game still burned, a reminder of the debt he was determined to settle.

Finally, the day arrived when Jebidiah's hard work paid off, and his pockets were full again. With a newfound sense of purpose, he challenged the man who had bested him all those years ago to a poker game for the ages, one that would see them both put everything on the line.

The stage was set, and the players gathered, anticipation crackling in the air like the charge before a storm. The two men locked eyes, each aware that the game would decide their fates. The cards were dealt, and the game began.

As the hours passed, Jebidiah and Diamond Jack matched each other in skill and cunning, their fortunes rising and falling like the tide. The onlookers watched with bated breath, unsure of which man would emerge victorious.

But in the end, the fates had other plans. For just as the game reached its climax, The Queen's Vengeance struck a hidden sandbar, sending the boat lurching onto its side. In the chaos that followed, the poker game was forgotten, as the passengers and crew scrambled to save themselves and the riverboat from certain destruction.

And so, the battle between Jebidiah McAllister and Diamond Jack would remain unresolved, their destinies intertwined by the river that had come to define their lives. For in the grand and ever-changing tapestry of the Mississippi, there are no simple endings, only the ceaseless flow of life's currents, forever forging new paths through the murky waters.

Screenplay

Title: The River's Gamble

copyright 2023 peacockOriginals.com LLC

INT. QUEEN'S VENGEANCE - POKER ROOM - NIGHT

A dimly lit room filled with the clinking of coins, smoky air, and the murmur of hushed conversations. At the center, JEBIDIAH MCALLISTER (30s, rugged) faces off against DIAMOND JACK (40s, sly) in an intense poker game. Jebidiah's fortune lies in the middle of the table. The tension is palpable.

EXT. QUEEN'S VENGEANCE - DECK - DAY

Jebidiah, now a deckhand, works tirelessly scrubbing the deck, hoisting cargo, and mending ropes. His brow is furrowed, and his face displays determination.

INT. QUEEN'S VENGEANCE - CAPTAIN'S QUARTERS - DAY

Captain HORATIO BARTHOLOMEW (60s, grizzled) instructs Jebidiah on the ways of the river, as Jebidiah listens attentively.

EXT. QUEEN'S VENGEANCE - DECK - EVENING

Jebidiah stands at the railing, staring at the setting sun. He looks contemplative, his thoughts focused on his plan.

INT. QUEEN'S VENGEANCE - POKER ROOM - NIGHT

The poker room is filled to the brim. Jebidiah and Diamond Jack face off once more, the stakes higher than ever. The crowd watches in anticipation.

EXT. QUEEN'S VENGEANCE - DAY

As the intense poker game continues inside, the riverboat strikes a hidden sandbar. The boat lurches violently.

INT. QUEEN'S VENGEANCE - POKER ROOM - DAY

Chaos ensues as passengers and crew rush to escape the sinking riverboat. The poker game, now insignificant, is abandoned in the commotion.

EXT. QUEEN'S VENGEANCE - DAY

Jebidiah and Diamond Jack, among others, cling to the wreckage of the riverboat, their rivalry unresolved. The mighty Mississippi flows around them, indifferent to their plight.

FADE OUT.

Shooting Script

Title: The River's Gamble

copyright 2023 peacockOriginals.com LLC

EXT. MISSISSIPPI RIVER - QUEEN'S VENGEANCE - NIGHT

The grand riverboat QUEEN'S VENGEANCE glides smoothly along the Mississippi River, her lights glowing in the darkness.

INT. QUEEN'S VENGEANCE - POKER ROOM - NIGHT

A dimly lit room, filled with the clinking of coins, smoky air, and the murmur of hushed conversations.

ANGLE ON: JEBIDIAH MCALLISTER (30s, rugged) and DIAMOND JACK (40s, sly) in a heated poker game. Jebidiah's entire fortune is at stake.

CLOSE-UP: The final card is revealed. Jebidiah has lost.

INT. QUEEN'S VENGEANCE - CREW QUARTERS - DAY

Jebidiah, now a deckhand, wakes up early and prepares for a long day of work.

EXT. QUEEN'S VENGEANCE - DECK - DAY

Jebidiah scrubs the deck, hoists cargo, and mends ropes with determination.

INT. QUEEN'S VENGEANCE - CAPTAIN'S QUARTERS - DAY

Captain HORATIO BARTHOLOMEW (60s, grizzled) instructs Jebidiah on the ways of the river.

EXT. QUEEN'S VENGEANCE - DECK - EVENING

Jebidiah gazes at the setting sun, deep in thought, as he hatches his plan.

INT. QUEEN'S VENGEANCE - POKER ROOM - NIGHT

The room is packed, buzzing with anticipation. Jebidiah and Diamond Jack face off once more, the stakes higher than ever.

CUT TO:

EXT. QUEEN'S VENGEANCE - DAY

The riverboat strikes a hidden sandbar.

INT. QUEEN'S VENGEANCE - POKER ROOM - DAY

Chaos ensues. Passengers and crew rush to escape the sinking riverboat, leaving the poker game abandoned.

EXT. QUEEN'S VENGEANCE - DAY

Jebidiah, Diamond Jack, and other survivors cling to the wreckage of the riverboat.

ANGLE ON: JEBIDIAH AND DIAMOND JACK

Their eyes meet briefly, the rivalry unresolved, before they both turn their attention to their immediate predicament.

FADE OUT.

Ocean Fortunes

[in the style of Herman Melville]

In the vast and stormy waters of the Pacific, aboard the good ship Nautilus, a motley crew of seafarers journeyed in search of adventure and prosperity. The ship's timbers creaked as it danced upon the waves, ever subject to the whims of the sea. It was a time when men braved the deep, driven by dreams of wealth and the romance of the ocean's terrible beauty.

The ship's captain, a hardy and experienced seaman named Obadiah, was no stranger to the dangers that lay beneath the surface. He had sailed upon the treacherous waves since the tender age of twelve, and had seen more than his fair share of calamity. Yet, the ocean's beauty held him in its thrall; each sunrise over the endless expanse of water, a reminder of the wonders that lay ahead.

One fateful day, as the crew sat gathered around the mess table, a strange object caught the eye of a young sailor named Ishmael. A fortune cookie, the likes of which had never before been seen on the Nautilus, lay before him. Its golden, crisp shell promised a glimpse into the mysteries of the future. With trembling hands, Ishmael cracked the cookie in twain, and a small strip of paper fell to the table.

"The ocean is a dangerous but beautiful place," he read aloud, as the crew stared in awe.

The words struck deep in their hearts, resonating with the unspoken truth of their souls. Each man knew the peril they faced, yet each was drawn to the sea's magnificence. They sailed on, the fortune cookie's prophecy ever present in their minds.

A fortnight later, the ship found itself ensnared in the throes of a fierce tempest. The winds howled and the waves crashed upon the deck, as the crew fought valiantly to keep the Nautilus afloat. Amidst the chaos, Captain Obadiah stood firm, issuing orders with a thunderous voice that matched the storm's fury.

As the storm intensified, so too did the crew's desperation. The sails were torn, and the ship's mast threatened to snap beneath the strain. All seemed lost as the watery abyss beckoned them towards their doom. In that moment, Ishmael recalled the fortune cookie's message, and a sense of calm enveloped him.

He cried out to the crew, reminding them of the ocean's beauty amidst the danger. His voice pierced through the gale, and one by one, the sailors found solace in the message. They redoubled their efforts, driven by the will to survive and the desire to witness once more the majesty of the sea.

With herculean effort, the crew managed to steer the ship through the storm, guided by the unwavering hand of Captain Obadiah. When the tempest finally abated, the Nautilus emerged battered but unbroken. The men stood upon the deck, gazing at the azure sky and the sea's tranquil surface, grateful for their deliverance.

From that day forth, the crew of the Nautilus sailed with renewed purpose, undeterred by the ocean's perils. The fortune cookie's message became their mantra, a constant reminder of the beauty that lay hidden beneath the danger. And so, they ventured forth into the unknown, hearts filled with a love for the sea that would endure to their dying breaths.

As the days stretched into weeks, the crew of the Nautilus forged a bond that only those who had faced the ocean's wrath could understand. They shared tales of their past exploits, and even the most hardened sailors found solace in the camaraderie of their shipmates. With each passing day, their devotion to the sea grew stronger, and the memory of the fortune cookie's message burned ever brighter in their hearts.

One moonlit night, Captain Obadiah summoned his crew to the deck. His eyes gleamed with the fire of ambition as he spoke of a fabled treasure that lay hidden in a remote and treacherous corner of the Pacific. The crew listened with bated breath, their hearts pounding with anticipation. The allure of the ocean's beauty had not diminished, but now it was joined by the promise of untold riches.

They set their course for this uncharted territory, driven by the twin passions of adventure and greed. The seas remained calm, as if in deference to the crew's newfound purpose. Every man aboard the Nautilus felt the thrill of the hunt, and their eyes gleamed with the prospect of the prize that awaited them.

As they neared their destination, the waters grew darker and more forbidding. The ocean's surface churned, and the ship was buffeted by a relentless current that threatened to tear it asunder. Yet, the crew remained steadfast, their faith in Captain Obadiah unshaken.

At long last, the Nautilus reached the X upon their tattered map. With a sense of foreboding, the sailors lowered a rowboat into the roiling waters, and a small party led by Captain Obadiah and Ishmael ventured forth to claim their prize.

Their journey took them to the heart of a treacherous reef, where jagged rocks jutted from the depths like the teeth of some monstrous leviathan. The rowboat strained against the current, but the men pressed on, undeterred by the imminent danger.

As they entered the heart of the reef, the water grew eerily calm. The men could sense the treasure's presence, as though it called to them from the depths. Captain Obadiah and Ishmael, with their harpoons at the ready, plunged into the water, leaving the rest of the party to guard the rowboat.

The pair dove deeper and deeper, the ocean's dark embrace tightening around them. Suddenly, in the gloom, they spotted the glint of gold. Their hearts raced as they swam towards the source of the shimmer, the treasure within their grasp. But as they neared it, a monstrous shadow loomed over them, a creature of the deep stirred by their intrusion.

A titanic octopus, its tentacles adorned with the bones of countless sailors who had perished in the reef, barred their path. Its eyes glowed with a malevolent intelligence, as though it guarded the treasure by some ancient and unholy pact. In that moment, the ocean's danger was laid bare, and the beauty that had once captivated the men seemed but a distant memory.

Undaunted, Captain Obadiah and Ishmael fought the beast, their harpoons flashing through the water. The struggle was fierce and terrible, a testament to the ocean's savage nature. But the fortune cookie's message echoed in their minds, reminding them of the ocean's beauty even as they faced their most perilous foe.

With a final, desperate thrust, Captain Obadiah's harpoon found its mark, piercing the monster's heart. The octopus, its reign of terror at an end, sank to the depths, releasing its claim on the treasure. The men, exhausted but triumphant, retrieved the gold and returned to the rowboat.

The crew of the Nautilus, their prize secured, set sail for home, their hearts heavy with the knowledge of the ocean's danger. Yet, they could not deny the beauty that had guided them through their perilous journey, and they swore to remember the fortune cookie's message for as long as they lived.

In the years that followed, the tale of Captain Obadiah and the crew of the Nautilus passed into legend, their exploits a testament to the ocean's terrible beauty. And as new generations of sailors braved the deep, they did so with the words of the fortune cookie etched upon their hearts: "The ocean is a dangerous but beautiful place."

Screenplay

Title: Ocean Fortunes

copyright 2023 peacockOriginals.com LLC

EXT. NAUTILUS SHIP - DAY

The Nautilus, a weathered ship, sails across the vast and stormy waters of the Pacific. The crew, a motley assortment of seafarers, work tirelessly to maintain the ship.

INT. NAUTILUS MESS HALL - DAY

The crew gathers around the mess table, eating and sharing stories. YOUNG ISHMAEL finds a fortune cookie and cracks it open.

ISHMAEL (reading aloud) The ocean is a dangerous but beautiful place.

The crew exchanges glances, the message resonating within them.

EXT. NAUTILUS SHIP - NIGHT - STORM

The Nautilus battles a fierce storm. CAPTAIN OBADIAH stands firm, shouting orders as the crew scrambles to save the ship. Ishmael remembers the fortune cookie's message, and it strengthens their resolve.

INT. NAUTILUS MESS HALL - DAY

The crew, now closer after their brush with death, shares stories of past adventures. Captain Obadiah tells them of a fabled treasure hidden in a remote and treacherous corner of the Pacific.

EXT. NAUTILUS SHIP - DAY

The Nautilus sails toward the uncharted territory, the crew focused on their mission.

EXT. UNCHARTED REEF - DAY

The Nautilus arrives at the treacherous reef. Captain Obadiah and Ishmael lead a small party in a rowboat towards the heart of the reef.

UNDERWATER - DAY

Captain Obadiah and Ishmael dive into the dark waters, harpoons in hand. They spot the glint of gold, but a monstrous OCTOPUS blocks their path.

Captain Obadiah and Ishmael battle the octopus, their harpoons flashing through the water. With a final thrust, Captain Obadiah kills the beast, and they claim the treasure.

EXT. NAUTILUS SHIP - DAY

The crew of the Nautilus, treasure secured, sets sail for home. As they sail away, they reflect on the ocean's danger and beauty, forever changed by their experiences.

FADE OUT.

THE END

Shooting Script

Title: Ocean Fortunes

copyright 2023 peacockOriginals.com LLC

EXT. NAUTILUS SHIP - DAY

Wide shot of the Nautilus sailing across the Pacific Ocean, vast and stormy waters surrounding it.

EXT. NAUTILUS SHIP - DECK - DAY

Medium shots of the crew working on the deck, tying ropes and adjusting sails.

INT. NAUTILUS MESS HALL - DAY

Wide shot of the crew gathered around the mess table, eating and sharing stories.

CLOSE-UP on Young Ishmael finding a fortune cookie.

INSERT: Fortune cookie cracked open, revealing a message.

ISHMAEL (reading aloud) The ocean is a dangerous but beautiful place.

CLOSE-UP shots of crew members exchanging glances.

EXT. NAUTILUS SHIP - NIGHT - STORM

Wide shot of the Nautilus battling a fierce storm, waves crashing against it.

Medium shot of Captain Obadiah standing firm, shouting orders. Crew members scramble to save the ship.

CLOSE-UP on Ishmael remembering the fortune cookie's message, his resolve strengthening.

INT. NAUTILUS MESS HALL - DAY

Medium shots of the crew, now closer after their brush with death, sharing stories. Captain Obadiah tells them of the fabled treasure.

EXT. NAUTILUS SHIP - DAY

Wide shot of the Nautilus sailing towards the uncharted territory, crew members focused on their mission.

EXT. UNCHARTED REEF - DAY

Wide shot of the Nautilus arriving at the treacherous reef. Captain Obadiah and Ishmael lead a small party in a rowboat towards the heart of the reef.

UNDERWATER - DAY

Point-of-view shots of Captain Obadiah and Ishmael diving into the dark waters, harpoons in hand.

CLOSE-UP of the glint of gold in the distance. The monstrous OCTOPUS appears, blocking their path.

Medium shots of Captain Obadiah and Ishmael battling the octopus, their harpoons flashing through the water.

CLOSE-UP of Captain Obadiah's final thrust, killing the beast. They claim the treasure.

EXT. NAUTILUS SHIP - DAY

Wide shot of the crew of the Nautilus, treasure secured, setting sail for home.

Medium shots of the crew members reflecting on the ocean's danger and beauty, their faces showing how they have been forever changed by their experiences.

FADE OUT.

THE END

Parisian Rain

[in the style of F. Scott Fitzgerald]

In the saturated heart of Paris, the April rains poured down upon the city with a relentless melancholy, drowning its cobblestone streets and flooding the Seine with sorrow. I had taken refuge in my small, dimly lit apartment, the damp walls and the deafening patter of rain outside my window, my only companions. I was a young writer, my heart filled with a hunger for life, but my pockets empty, and my hands stained with ink and disillusionment.

It was in the midst of this despair, as the rain continued to cascade down upon the city, that I found myself in the Café de Flore, a beacon of life and conversation, tucked away in the Saint-Germain-des-Prés. I had taken my usual seat, a secluded corner with a view of the melancholic streets, and had submerged myself in the pages of my latest manuscript.

Suddenly, the door of the café opened with a gust of wind and a cascade of raindrops, and she stepped in – a vision of beauty, clad in an elegant, tailored overcoat, her eyes hidden behind a pair of black sunglasses. Her raven hair clung to her porcelain cheeks like the tendrils of a vine, her lips a crimson promise.

As she removed her sunglasses, I found myself mesmerized by her gaze – a pair of emerald eyes that seemed to possess an otherworldly intensity. I could not help but feel that we were bound by some unseen force, that the fates had conspired to draw us together. She took a seat at the bar, her movements so graceful, so fluid, that she seemed to float across the room.

For several stormy days, I observed her from a distance, her presence in the café both a source of enchantment and despair. I longed to approach her, to speak with her, but I was paralyzed by my own insecurity – a struggling writer, with little more than ink-stained dreams to offer. And yet, I felt certain that she was aware of my gaze, that she was waiting for me to take the first step.

Finally, one evening, as the rain continued to pelt the windows of the café, I mustered the courage to approach her. My heart pounded in my chest as I walked towards her, each step a battle against my own fear.

"Bonjour, Mademoiselle," I stuttered, my voice barely audible above the din of conversation and the relentless rain.

"Bonjour," she replied, her voice a melody that seemed to echo through my very soul.

And so, our story began. Her name was Greta, a German émigré who had come to Paris in search of a new life. She spoke of her love for literature and art, her fascination with the city's rich history and vibrant culture. I was entranced, both by her beauty and her intellect, and I found myself falling in love with her as we spent our days wandering the rain-soaked streets of Paris, our conversations as deep and mysterious as the swollen river that flowed through the heart of the city.

But as the weeks passed, I began to sense that there was a darkness hidden within her, a secret that she could not, or would not, reveal. She would disappear for hours, sometimes days at a time, returning with a haunted look in her eyes, her lips sealed by an unspoken truth.

One fateful evening, I followed her through the narrow streets of Paris, my heart heavy with a mixture of fear and longing. She led me to a shadowy alley, where she met with a man whose face was obscured by a fedora and a cloak. They exchanged whispers, their words unintelligible, before she handed him a small, leather-bound book, and received a similar one from him.

As they parted, I confronted her, my heart aching with a sense of betrayal. "What is this, Greta? Who is that man?" I demanded, my voice trembling with emotion.

She looked at me, her emerald eyes filled with a sadness I had never seen before. "Please, Pierre, I cannot tell you. Just know that I have no choice," she whispered, her voice barely audible above the rain that continued to pour down around us.

Desperate for answers, I seized the leather-bound book from her trembling hands and opened it, my heart pounding in my chest. To my horror, I discovered that it was filled with detailed maps, codes, and military intelligence – secrets that could alter the course of the war. Greta was a spy, and I, a foolish writer, had fallen in love with her.

"I am so sorry, Pierre," she said, her voice a choked sob. "I never meant for you to find out like this. I wanted to tell you, but I couldn't risk your safety."

As I stood there, the cold rain drenching my body, I realized that I was faced with a decision that would change the course of our lives forever. I could expose her secret, or I could protect her, risking my own life in the process. I chose weakness.

In that moment, my love for her outweighed the danger, and I made my choice. I pulled her into my arms, our lips meeting in a passionate embrace, the rain washing away our tears.

From that day forward, we navigated the treacherous waters of war and deception together, our love a beacon in the darkness, a shelter from the storm. As the city of Paris continued to be battered by the relentless rain, our love remained a constant, unyielding force, defying the odds and the perils that threatened to tear us apart.

And so, we danced beneath the stormy skies, our hearts entwined, our love a testament to the power of human connection – a love born amidst the chaos of war and a seemingly endless rainy season.

As the months passed, Greta and I became increasingly adept at navigating the treacherous world of espionage. We communicated in secret codes, our words and glances concealing hidden meanings, our love a fortress against the ever-present danger that surrounded us.

In those stolen moments, we would escape the shadows of war, losing ourselves in the beauty of Paris – the flickering gas lamps that cast their golden glow upon the rain-soaked streets, the haunting melodies of an accordion echoing through the night, the sweet scent of lilacs that lingered in the air as the city prepared to bloom anew.

But with each passing day, the risk grew greater, the noose of suspicion tightening around our necks. We knew that it was only a matter of time before our secret was discovered, and we were torn apart.

It was a cold, rainy evening when the moment we had feared finally arrived. As I returned to our small apartment, I found the door ajar, a foreboding sense of dread filling the air. I entered cautiously, my heart pounding in my chest, and discovered Greta bound to a chair, her emerald eyes filled with terror.

Before I could react, a man emerged from the shadows, a pistol aimed at my heart. "You have been very clever, Monsieur," he said, his voice cold and emotionless. "But your luck has run out."

As I stared into the face of death, I knew that I had but one final decision to make – to save the woman I loved, or to die in the attempt. Without hesitation, I lunged at the man, my fingers grasping for the pistol, my heart fueled by a love that transcended fear and despair.

In the chaos that ensued, a single shot rang out, echoing through the rain-soaked streets like a thunderclap. The man slumped to the floor, the pistol slipping from his lifeless fingers, and I knew that our love had triumphed over the darkness that had threatened to consume us.

As I untied Greta, her body trembling with a mixture of relief and fear, I looked into her eyes and saw that our love had been forever changed – forged in the fires of war, and tempered by the relentless rain that had fallen upon our city.

We fled Paris that night, our hearts heavy with the knowledge that we would never again walk its cobblestone streets, or lose ourselves in the beauty of its rain-soaked alleys. But as we embraced beneath the stormy skies, we knew that our love had become something greater than ourselves – a testament to the resilience of the human spirit, and the enduring power of love in the face of adversity.

And so, we walked hand in hand into the darkness, the rain a gentle caress upon our skin, our love a beacon that would guide us through the storm and into the dawn of a new day.

Screenplay

Title: Parisian Rain

copyright 2023 peacockOriginals.com LLC

INT. PARISIAN APARTMENT - DAY

Pierre, a young Parisian writer, sits at a small desk, engrossed in his manuscript. The sound of heavy rain echoes throughout the dimly lit apartment.

EXT. CAFÉ DE FLORE - DAY

Rain pours down on the streets of Paris. Pierre enters the bustling café, shaking off his umbrella before taking his usual seat in a secluded corner.

INT. CAFÉ DE FLORE - DAY

Pierre watches as Greta, a beautiful, mysterious woman, enters the café. Their eyes lock, and Pierre is immediately captivated.

INT. CAFÉ DE FLORE - NIGHT

After several days of observing Greta, Pierre finally musters the courage to approach her.

PIERRE Bonjour, Mademoiselle.

GRETA Bonjour.

Over time, their romance blossoms as they explore Paris together, sharing conversations about literature, art, and culture.

EXT. PARIS STREETS - NIGHT

Pierre, filled with suspicion, follows Greta to a shadowy alley where she meets a mysterious man.

INT. SHADOWY ALLEY - NIGHT

Pierre confronts Greta about her secret meeting and the leather-bound book filled with military intelligence.

PIERRE What is this, Greta? Who is that man?

GRETA (tearful) Please, Pierre, I cannot tell you. Just know that I have no choice.

Pierre decides to protect Greta and their love, pulling her into a passionate embrace.

INT. PARISIAN APARTMENT - NIGHT

Pierre discovers Greta, bound and terrified, with a man pointing a gun at him.

PIERRE (enraged) Let her go!

Pierre lunges at the man, and in the struggle, a gunshot rings out.

INT. PARISIAN APARTMENT - NIGHT

With the danger now passed, Pierre and Greta realize their love has been forever changed. They decide to flee Paris together.

EXT. PARIS STREETS - NIGHT

Hand in hand, Pierre and Greta walk into the darkness, leaving the rain-soaked streets of Paris behind.

FADE OUT.

Shooting Script

Title: Parisian Rain

copyright 2023 peacockOriginals.com LLC

INT. PARISIAN APARTMENT - DAY

CLOSE UP on Pierre's ink-stained hands as he writes in his manuscript. PULL BACK to reveal Pierre at his small desk in the dimly lit apartment. The sound of heavy rain outside.

CUT TO:

EXT. CAFÉ DE FLORE - DAY

Rain pours down on the streets of Paris. Pierre enters the bustling café, shaking off his umbrella before taking his usual seat in a secluded corner.

CUT TO:

INT. CAFÉ DE FLORE - DAY

ANGLE ON Pierre as he watches Greta enter the café. Their eyes lock, and Pierre is immediately captivated. CUT to Greta removing her sunglasses, revealing her mesmerizing eyes.

CUT TO:

INT. CAFÉ DE FLORE - NIGHT

ANGLE ON Pierre as he takes a deep breath, mustering the courage to approach Greta.

PIERRE Bonjour, Mademoiselle.

GRETA (smiling) Bonjour.

CUT TO:

EXT. PARIS STREETS - MONTAGE

A series of shots showing Pierre and Greta exploring Paris together, sharing conversations about literature, art, and culture, as their romance blossoms.

CUT TO:

EXT. PARIS STREETS - NIGHT

ANGLE ON Pierre, filled with suspicion, as he follows Greta to a shadowy alley.

CUT TO:

INT. SHADOWY ALLEY - NIGHT

Pierre confronts Greta about her secret meeting with the MYSTERIOUS MAN and the leather-bound book filled with military intelligence.

PIERRE (angry) What is this, Greta? Who is that man?

GRETA (tearful) Please, Pierre, I cannot tell you. Just know that I have no choice.

CUT TO:

INT. SHADOWY ALLEY - NIGHT

CLOSE UP on Pierre as he makes the decision to protect Greta and their love. He pulls her into a passionate embrace.

CUT TO:

INT. PARISIAN APARTMENT - NIGHT

Pierre enters the apartment to find Greta, bound and terrified. The MYSTERIOUS MAN points a gun at him.

PIERRE (enraged) Let her go!

CUT TO:

INT. PARISIAN APARTMENT - NIGHT

Pierre lunges at the MYSTERIOUS MAN. CLOSE UP on Pierre's hand grabbing for the gun. A gunshot rings out.

CUT TO:

INT. PARISIAN APARTMENT - NIGHT

The MYSTERIOUS MAN lies motionless on the floor. Pierre frees Greta. They realize their love has been forever changed and decide to flee Paris together.

CUT TO:

EXT. PARIS STREETS - NIGHT

Hand in hand, Pierre and Greta walk into the darkness, leaving the rain-soaked streets of Paris behind. The rain continues to pour.

FADE OUT.

Coco Loco Moco

[in the style of Ernest Hemingway]

In the days before the war, there was a man who went by the name of Benjamin. He was a tall, lean man with a face that seemed to hold the memories of a thousand lifetimes. He had been many things in his life, but now he was only a bartender, and a purveyor of dreams and nightmares.

Benjamin had come to Key West in the spring, with the sky the color of a robin's egg, and the sea that stretched out before him like a great blue desert. He had been drawn to the island, by the stories of a mysterious, lost treasure. But what he found was something far more precious, and infinitely more rare.

He bought an old, weather-beaten bar on the outskirts of town, with floors that groaned beneath his feet and windows that rattled in the wind. He painted the walls a deep, dark blue, the color of the ocean at midnight, and hung fishing nets and old nautical maps upon them. The bar had been many things before – a brothel, a gambling den, a church – but now it was a sanctuary, a place where men and women could come and share their stories, their dreams, and their nightmares.

It was in this place that Benjamin discovered the secret of the Coco Loco Moco – a drink that was said to have been born in the heart of the Maui, and island in Hawai'i, a concoction so powerful that it could unlock the hidden depths of a man's soul. He had found the recipe in an old leather-bound book, and he spent long nights perfecting the blend of rum, coconut milk, pineapple juice, and the secret ingredient that would give the drink its power.

The Coco Loco Moco was not a drink for everyone. It was a drink for those who were brave enough to face their fears, and their desires. It was a drink for those who longed to escape the world, if only for a moment, and find themselves lost in the wild, untamed landscape of their own dreams.

One by one, they came to Benjamin's bar, drawn by the stories that had begun to spread through the island like wildfire. They came from all walks of life – fishermen, artists, sailors, and drifters – each with a tale to tell, and a thirst that only the Coco Loco Moco could quench.

There was the old man who had lost his son to the sea, and who now spent his days searching the horizon for a glimpse of the ship that had taken him away. There was the young woman who had come to Key West to escape a loveless marriage, only to find herself trapped in the nightmare of her own making. And there was the boy who had left his home in the North, seeking adventure and fortune, but who had found only loneliness and despair.

Night after night, they would gather at Benjamin's bar, sipping their Coco Loco Mocos and sharing their stories. And as they drank, their fears and their dreams would rise to the surface, like ghosts from the depths of the sea. They would speak of their hopes and their regrets, their loves and their losses, and through their words, they would find solace and redemption, and inevitably another drink.

For in the end, it was not the Coco Loco Moco that held the power to heal their broken hearts, but the act of sharing their stories. It was in the telling of their tales, and the listening of others, that they found the strength to face their fears and embrace their dreams.

And as for Benjamin, he became not just a bartender, but a keeper of secrets, a collector of memories, and a guardian of the dreams, and nightmares, that haunted the hearts of those who came to his bar. And in the twilight of his own life, as he stood on the shores of Key West and watched the sun sink below the horizon, he knew that he had found his own treasure – not in the form of gold or silver, but in the stories of the people who had come to share their lives with him.

Years passed, and the legend of Benjamin's bar and the Coco Loco Moco continued to grow. People traveled from far and wide to taste the mysterious drink and unburden their souls. And as the stories were shared, the walls of the bar seemed to absorb them, until it was as if the very building itself was alive with the dreams and sorrows of those who had come before.

But time is a relentless master, and even Benjamin could not escape its grasp. His hair grew thin and white, his face etched with the lines of a thousand stories, and his once-strong hands now trembled as he mixed the Coco Loco Moco.

One evening, as the sun dipped beneath the waves and the sky was painted with the colors of twilight, a stranger came to the bar. He was a man of indeterminate age, with a face that seemed both young and old, and eyes that held the glimmer of distant stars.

He took a seat at the bar and ordered a Coco Loco Moco. As he sipped the drink, his eyes met Benjamin's, and in that moment, it was as if the two men shared a secret understanding – a connection that transcended time and space.

"Tell me your story, Benjamin," the stranger said, his voice soft and lilting. "Tell me of your dreams, and of your nightmares."

And so, for the first time in his life, Benjamin found himself on the other side of the bar, sharing his own story with the stranger. He spoke of his youth, his wanderings, and his search for treasure. He spoke of the people he had met, and the stories he had heard. And as he spoke, he felt a great weight lifting from his heart, as if the ghosts of his past were finally being set free.

When he had finished, the stranger smiled and said, "You have done well, Benjamin. You have given these people a place to share their stories, and in doing so, you have eased their burdens. But now it is time for you to rest, and to let others carry on your work."

With that, the stranger stood and left the bar, disappearing into the night as quickly as he had come. And as the last light of day faded from the sky, Benjamin somehow knew, even felt it in his old bones, that his time had come.

He closed the bar for the last time, leaving behind the stories, that he had collected over the years. And as he walked away, he knew that his treasure would live on, not in the walls of the bar or the depths of the sea, but in the hearts of those who had come to share their lives with him.

And in the very coconuts that yearned from the tallest palms, hoping to be a part of the next round.

Screenplay

Title: Coco Loco Moco

copyright 2023 peacockOriginals.com LLC

FADE IN:

EXT. KEY WEST - DAY

A vibrant island paradise, with clear blue skies and the sea stretching out like a great blue desert. Seagulls fly overhead, and palm trees sway in the breeze.

INT. BENJAMIN'S BAR - DAY

A dimly lit, weather-beaten bar on the outskirts of town, with floors that groan and windows that rattle. The walls are adorned with fishing nets and old nautical maps.

BENJAMIN (40s), tall, lean, with a face that holds the memories of a thousand lifetimes, stands behind the bar, mixing a Coco Loco Moco.

OLD MAN (70s), weary and weathered, sits at the bar, nursing his drink.

OLD MAN My son was lost to the sea, you know. I come here to search for him.

BENJAMIN I've heard many stories, but the sea keeps her secrets close.

YOUNG WOMAN (30s), with a haunted look in her eyes, enters the bar and takes a seat.

YOUNG WOMAN I need a Coco Loco Moco. I've heard it can help me forget.

BENJAMIN (serving her the drink) It can open the doors to your soul, but only you can choose to step through.

As the Young Woman takes a sip, her eyes close, and she seems transported to another place.

INT. BENJAMIN'S BAR - NIGHT

Over the years, the bar has become a sanctuary for those who need it, and a place to share stories. Benjamin stands behind the bar, listening to the patrons' tales.

INT. BENJAMIN'S BAR - NIGHT (YEARS LATER)

Benjamin, now older, with white hair and a lined face, continues to serve Coco Loco Mocos and listen to the stories of the patrons.

A STRANGER (ageless, with eyes that hold the glimmer of distant stars) enters the bar and takes a seat.

STRANGER Give me a Coco Loco Moco, Benjamin. And then tell me your story.

BENJAMIN (surprised) My story? I've never told it before.

STRANGER (smiling) It's time.

Benjamin takes a deep breath and begins sharing his own story with the Stranger. The other patrons listen intently.

EXT. KEY WEST - DUSK

The sun sets, painting the sky in the colors of twilight. The Stranger exits the bar and vanishes into the night.

INT. BENJAMIN'S BAR - NIGHT

Benjamin, now at peace, closes the bar for the last time. He walks away, leaving behind the stories, dreams, and nightmares he has collected.

FADE OUT:

THE END

Shooting Script

Title: Coco Loco Moco

copyright 2023 peacockOriginals.com LLC

FADE IN:

EXT. KEY WEST - DAY

A1. Establishing shot of the island paradise, with clear blue skies, the sea stretching out like a great blue desert, seagulls flying overhead, and palm trees swaying in the breeze.

INT. BENJAMIN'S BAR - DAY

B1. Wide shot of the dimly lit, weather-beaten bar with floors that groan and windows that rattle. The walls are adorned with fishing nets and old nautical maps.

B2. Medium shot of BENJAMIN (40s), tall, lean, with a face that holds the memories of a thousand lifetimes, standing behind the bar, mixing a Coco Loco Moco.

B3. Close-up of the OLD MAN (70s), weary and weathered, sitting at the bar, nursing his drink.

OLD MAN My son was lost to the sea, you know. I come here to search for him.

B4. Reverse shot of Benjamin, nodding.

BENJAMIN I've heard many stories, but the sea keeps her secrets close.

B5. Wide shot of the YOUNG WOMAN (30s), with a haunted look in her eyes, entering the bar and taking a seat.

YOUNG WOMAN I need a Coco Loco Moco. I've heard it can help me forget.

B6. Medium shot of Benjamin, serving her the drink.

BENJAMIN It can open the doors to your soul, but only you can choose to step through.

B7. Close-up of the Young Woman taking a sip, her eyes close, and she seems transported to another place.

INT. BENJAMIN'S BAR - NIGHT (MONTAGE)

C1. Montage of various shots of patrons in the bar over the years, sharing their stories with Benjamin as he serves Coco Loco Mocos.

INT. BENJAMIN'S BAR - NIGHT (YEARS LATER)

D1. Wide shot of the bar, now with an older Benjamin, his hair white and face lined, still serving Coco Loco Mocos and listening to the patrons' stories.

D2. Medium shot of the STRANGER (ageless, with eyes that hold the glimmer of distant stars) entering the bar and taking a seat.

STRANGER Give me a Coco Loco Moco, Benjamin. And then tell me your story.

D3. Close-up of Benjamin, surprised.

BENJAMIN My story? I've never told it before.

D4. Medium shot of the Stranger, smiling.

STRANGER It's time.

D5. Wide shot of Benjamin taking a deep breath and beginning to share his story, as the other patrons listen intently.

EXT. KEY WEST - DUSK

E1. Establishing shot of the sun setting, painting the sky in the colors of twilight.

E2. Medium shot of the Stranger exiting the bar and vanishing into the night.

INT. BENJAMIN'S BAR - NIGHT

F1. Wide shot of Benjamin, now at peace, closing the bar for the last time.

F2. Close-up of Benjamin's face, filled with emotion.

F3. Wide shot of Benjamin walking away from the bar, leaving behind the stories, dreams, and nightmares he has collected.

FADE OUT:

THE END

The Elysian Gale

[in the style of Edgar Allen Poe]

Once upon a midday dreary, in the cold and misty docks of Boston, our tale begins with a young woman of exquisite beauty and spirit, one Eliza Montgomery. The year was 1813, and the world seemed to tremble with the promise of a new age. Eliza, desperate to escape the drudgery of her life in the city, sought solace upon a vessel bound for the verdant shores of Jamaica. Little did she know that her destiny would be altered irreversibly by the tempestuous embrace of the sea.

A vessel of the finest craftsmanship, the "The Elysian Gale" stood proudly against the crashing waves, its hull glistening in the moonlight. As the ship's timbers creaked and moaned with the weight of their precious cargo, the passengers aboard whispered of the legends of fortune that awaited them in the sun-kissed lands of the Caribbean.

Three days hence, the skies darkened, and a storm of unnatural ferocity bore down upon the "The Elysian Gale." The ship's crew fought valiantly against the raging tempest, as thunderous roars echoed through the night, shattering the illusion of safety the passengers had held so dear. The howling winds tore at their very souls, while the waves clawed mercilessly at the ship's hull, threatening to tear her asunder.

In the darkest hour of the tempest's fury, the ship's master, Captain O'Brien, ordered the crew to scuttle the "The Elysian Gale" off the coast of Georgia, lest they all be consigned to the cold and unforgiving embrace of the deep. To the lifeboats, they fled, with Eliza Montgomery among them, fear and despair etched upon her angelic countenance.

Through the maelstrom, the lifeboats were cast ashore, their desperate occupants huddling together for warmth and solace. The storm abated, leaving the survivors to survey their desolate surroundings. Eliza, her indomitable spirit unbroken, saw the fertile soil beneath her feet and the verdant, untouched land that spread out before her as a canvas upon which she would paint her destiny.

With determination and grit, she resolved to build a life anew amidst the cotton fields of Georgia. And so, the seeds of her legacy were sown. Over time, the cotton plantation she established flourished, nourished by her unwavering spirit and the blood, sweat, and tears of those who toiled under her command.

Through the decades, her dynasty grew, the Montgomery name becoming synonymous with wealth and power in the South. As the cotton industry expanded, so too did the empire that she had forged from the storm-tossed wreckage of her former life. For one hundred years, her descendants would carry on her legacy, their wealth and influence spreading like tendrils across the nation.

But as the saying goes, all good things must come to an end. As the sun began to set on the Montgomery dynasty, so too did the shadows of history encroach upon its once-mighty halls. For in the heart of every great empire, there lies a darkness that cannot be escaped, a specter of ruin that waits patiently for the moment to strike.

And so, the winds of change would sweep once more through the lands that had been shaped by the indomitable spirit of Eliza Montgomery. The world would move on, leaving behind the crumbling remains of a once-great dynasty, a testament to the impermanence of fortune and the relentless march of time.

Yet, the spirit of Eliza Montgomery would live on, for her tale is one of resilience and determination, a story that speaks to the very core of the human experience. Her legacy, though marred by the ravages of time and the inexorable march of history, stands as a testament to the power of the human spirit to endure and overcome adversity. And though the grandeur of her empire may have faded, her name would be forever etched into the annals of time.

For generations to come, the story of Eliza Montgomery and her cotton dynasty would be told and retold, passed down from parent to child, woven into the very fabric of the land upon which her empire once stood. Her tale would serve as both a cautionary reminder of the fleeting nature of wealth and power, and an inspiration for those who sought to forge their own path in the face of adversity.

As the echoes of her name reverberated through time, a quiet, melancholic beauty seemed to envelop the lands she had once tamed. The cotton fields, now wild and untamed, whispered her story to the winds that gently rustled through their leaves. The once-grand Montgomery estate, now reclaimed by nature, stood as a haunting reminder of a bygone era, its silent halls echoing with the distant laughter and tears of generations past.

And as the seasons passed and the years rolled by, the spirit of Eliza Montgomery would become a part of the land itself, her indomitable spirit woven into the very fabric of the earth that had nurtured her dreams and aspirations. In the wind, the rain, and the gentle rustle of cotton leaves, her presence would be felt, a whisper of a time when the world seemed to tremble with the promise of a new age.

For Eliza Montgomery, the young woman who had once escaped the confines of Boston upon the storm-tossed waves of the sea, her story was one of resilience, of triumph over adversity, and of the enduring power of the human spirit. And though her empire may have crumbled, her legacy would live on, a beacon of hope for those who dared to dream amidst the ever-shifting sands of time.

Screenplay

Title: The Elysian Gale

copyright 2023 peacockOriginals.com LLC

INT. BOSTON DOCKS - NIGHT

The misty docks of Boston are dimly lit. ELIZA MONTGOMERY, a young woman of exquisite beauty and spirit, stands at the edge of the dock, staring at the ship, "Maiden's Voyage."

EXT. MAIDEN'S VOYAGE - NIGHT

The ship creaks and moans as the passengers board. Eliza joins them, looking back at the city she is leaving behind.

EXT. MAIDEN'S VOYAGE - OPEN SEA - DAY

Three days into the journey, the skies darken. A storm approaches, and the ship's crew works feverishly to prepare.

INT. MAIDEN'S VOYAGE - NIGHT

The storm rages outside. Eliza and the passengers huddle together, terrified. CAPTAIN O'BRIEN enters.

CAPTAIN O'BRIEN (Shouting) We must scuttle the ship! To the lifeboats!

The passengers and crew scramble to the lifeboats, abandoning the "Maiden's Voyage."

EXT. GEORGIA COAST - DAY

The survivors, including Eliza, are washed ashore. Exhausted and frightened, they survey their new surroundings.

ELIZA (Determined) We will build a life anew here.

EXT. GEORGIA COTTON PLANTATION - DAY

Eliza stands in a flourishing cotton field, surveying the plantation she has built.

EXT. MONTGOMERY ESTATE - DAY - YEARS LATER

The plantation has grown. Eliza's descendants now run the thriving cotton empire.

INT. MONTGOMERY ESTATE - DAY

The once-great estate is now empty and crumbling. The Montgomery dynasty is coming to an end.

EXT. GEORGIA COTTON FIELDS - DAY

The cotton fields have grown wild and untamed, whispering Eliza's story to the winds.

FADE OUT:

THE END

Shooting Script

Title: The Elysian Gale

copyright 2023 peacockOriginals.com LLC

Scene 1: Boston Docks

EXT. BOSTON DOCKS - NIGHT

1.1 Wide shot of misty docks, dimly lit, with the "Maiden's Voyage" in the background.

1.2 Medium shot of ELIZA MONTGOMERY standing at the edge of the dock, staring at the ship.

Scene 2: Boarding the Ship

EXT. MAIDEN'S VOYAGE - NIGHT

2.1 Wide shot of passengers boarding the ship.

2.2 Close-up of Eliza boarding, looking back at the city.

Scene 3: The Storm

EXT. MAIDEN'S VOYAGE - OPEN SEA - DAY

3.1 Establishing shot of dark skies, storm approaching.

3.2 Close-up of crew members working to prepare the ship.

INT. MAIDEN'S VOYAGE - NIGHT

3.3 Medium shot of frightened passengers huddled together.

3.4 Medium shot of CAPTAIN O'BRIEN entering, shouting.

CAPTAIN O'BRIEN (Shouting) We must scuttle the ship! To the lifeboats!

3.5 Montage of passengers and crew scrambling to the lifeboats.

Scene 4: Washed Ashore

EXT. GEORGIA COAST - DAY

4.1 Wide shot of survivors washed ashore, exhausted and frightened.

4.2 Close-up of Eliza, determined.

ELIZA (Determined) We will build a life anew here.

Scene 5: The Plantation

EXT. GEORGIA COTTON PLANTATION - DAY

5.1 Wide shot of Eliza standing in a flourishing cotton field.

5.2 Close-up of Eliza, surveying the plantation.

Scene 6: The Montgomery Estate

EXT. MONTGOMERY ESTATE - DAY - YEARS LATER

6.1 Establishing shot of the thriving Montgomery Estate.

INT. MONTGOMERY ESTATE - DAY

6.2 Medium shot of the once-great estate, now empty and crumbling.

Scene 7: The End

EXT. GEORGIA COTTON FIELDS - DAY

7.1 Wide shot of wild, untamed cotton fields.

7.2 Close-up of cotton leaves, whispering Eliza's story to the winds.

FADE OUT:

THE END

Magnolia Springs

[in the style of Harper Lee]

In the small town of Magnolia Springs, deep in the heart of the South, there stood an old diner. It was an unassuming building, no bigger than a one-room schoolhouse, with peeling white paint and a neon sign that read "Lilly's Diner." Despite its shabby exterior, the diner was the heart of the town, where the townsfolk gathered each morning for steaming cups of coffee and plates of biscuits and gravy.

In this simple place, a young white woman named Jean Louise worked as a waitress. She was a beautiful girl of eighteen with a head of golden curls and a heart full of dreams. Jean Louise had grown up in Magnolia Springs, surrounded by the usual small-town gossip and prejudices that come with life in the South.

One day, a stranger walked into Lilly's Diner. He was a Japanese salesman named Hiroshi, a middle-aged man with silver-streaked hair and a quiet air of dignity. Hiroshi had come to Magnolia Springs to sell his wares, for he represented a company that produced delicate and exquisite Japanese pottery. His arrival turned heads, for people of his heritage were a rarity in this part of the world.

As Jean Louise served Hiroshi a plate of fried chicken and collard greens, she found herself drawn to the man's gentle nature and the stories he told of his homeland. The more she listened, the more she came to appreciate the beauty and grace of his culture. It was not long before their conversations turned into something more, as the two found themselves falling in love.

The relationship between Jean Louise and Hiroshi was not without its difficulties. The townsfolk of Magnolia Springs were quick to cast judgment on the unusual couple, and whispers of disapproval echoed through the diner's walls. But Jean Louise's love for Hiroshi was stronger than any prejudice, and it was in his eyes that she saw the world she had always dreamed of.

As the months passed, Hiroshi began teaching Jean Louise about the art of Japanese pottery. They spent hours together, their hands molding the cool clay into intricate shapes as they shaped their love for one another. In the quiet moments, Jean Louise would gaze at Hiroshi's strong hands and imagine a life far away from Magnolia Springs, where they could live in peace.

One evening, as Jean Louise and Hiroshi walked hand in hand through the moonlit streets of Magnolia Springs, they came upon the old oak tree that stood in the center of town. The tree had been there for centuries, its branches reaching out like the arms of a wise old friend. It was here that Hiroshi asked Jean Louise to marry him, and she said yes without hesitation.

The news of their engagement was met with surprise and outrage. Many of the townspeople, including Jean Louise's own family, refused to accept their union, for they were blinded by their own prejudice. But Jean Louise knew that her love for Hiroshi was true, and she was determined to stand by his side.

On the day of their wedding, the small church was filled with friends and neighbors, some of whom still wore expressions of disapproval. Jean Louise, dressed in a simple white gown, walked down the aisle with her head held high, her eyes locked on Hiroshi's gentle gaze. As they exchanged their vows, the church bells rang out, signaling a new chapter in their lives.

Together, Jean Louise and Hiroshi left Magnolia Springs, eager to build a life far from the judgment of others. They traveled to Japan, where they opened a small pottery shop in a coastal village. It was there that they continued their work, creating beautiful pieces that reflected their love for one another and their commitment to overcoming the boundaries that had once threatened to tear them apart.

In the quiet moments of their life, as the sun set over the ocean and the scent of cherry blossoms filled the air, Jean Louise would think back to her days at Lilly's Diner. She would remember the whispers of disapproval and the sting of prejudice, and she would marvel at how far she had come. For in Hiroshi's arms, she had found a love that transcended the limitations of her small Southern town, and it was in that love that she had found her true home.

Years passed, and Jean Louise and Hiroshi's love only grew stronger. They raised two beautiful children, who were the embodiment of their love and the bridge between their cultures. The children learned to appreciate both their Japanese and Southern heritage, carrying on the legacy of their parents' brave and passionate love.

Word of the couple's success in Japan eventually reached Magnolia Springs, and slowly, the town's attitude began to change. Some of those who had once shunned Jean Louise and Hiroshi came to understand the power of love and the beauty of embracing different cultures. They realized that the color of one's skin or the land of one's birth did not define a person, but rather, it was the content of their character and the strength of their heart.

In the twilight of their lives, Jean Louise and Hiroshi returned to Magnolia Springs, their hands still intertwined and their love as strong as ever. They found the town had changed, as a new generation had begun to tear down the walls of prejudice that had once divided them. The old oak tree still stood in the center of town, its branches now stretched out in a welcoming embrace.

As Jean Louise and Hiroshi sat beneath the tree, they knew that their love had made a difference, not only in their lives but in the lives of those who had come to understand the beauty of acceptance. The legacy of their love would forever be etched in the hearts of those who had witnessed it, a testament to the power of love to overcome even the deepest and darkest of prejudices.

The sun shone bright on the day of Hiroshi's funeral, casting a warm light on the mourners who had gathered to pay their respects. They had come from near and far, a testament to the lives Hiroshi had touched with his gentle nature and his beautiful pottery. Jean Louise, now a silver-haired woman, stood by the graveside, her heart heavy with grief, but also filled with gratitude for the years of love they had shared.

The service was a blend of Japanese and Southern traditions, reflecting the rich tapestry of Hiroshi and Jean Louise's life together. Their children, now grown and with families of their own, spoke of their father's wisdom, his kindness, and the lessons he had taught them about love and acceptance. Friends from Magnolia Springs and their adopted village in Japan shared stories of Hiroshi's generosity and the way he had brought people together through his art.

As the ceremony concluded, a gentle breeze stirred the leaves of the old oak tree, as if Hiroshi's spirit was whispering a final goodbye. Jean Louise stepped forward, holding a small clay pot crafted by her husband's skilled hands. It was one of the first pieces they had made together, symbolizing the love that had blossomed between them.

With tears in her eyes, Jean Louise knelt beside the grave and tenderly placed the pot next to the headstone. As she stood up, she felt the warmth of the sun on her face and a sense of peace filled her heart. Though Hiroshi was no longer with her in body, she knew that their love would live on, carried forward by their children and the countless lives they had touched.

In the days and weeks that followed, Jean Louise found solace in the familiar rhythm of the pottery wheel. With each piece she created, she poured her love and her memories of Hiroshi into the clay, crafting tributes to the life they had shared. The people of Magnolia Springs, now a more open and accepting community, embraced her work, and the beautiful pottery became a symbol of the love story that had forever changed their town.

As the years went by, Jean Louise continued to share her and Hiroshi's story with future generations. Their love, once a source of controversy, had become a beacon of hope, showing that even in the darkest of times, love could triumph over prejudice and fear.

Under the watchful gaze of the old oak tree, Jean Louise would sit and reflect on her life with Hiroshi. And though her heart still ached with the pain of his loss, she knew that their love would never truly die. It lived on in the branches of the tree, in the hearts of their children, and in the legacy of their love that had transformed not just their lives, but the lives of all who had known them.

The passage of time had softened the pain of Hiroshi's passing, leaving Jean Louise with a quiet sense of longing for a new beginning. She had heard stories of San Francisco, a city where East met West, and she felt a pull toward the distant shores that had shaped her beloved husband. With her children's encouragement, Jean Louise decided to embark on a journey, both to honor Hiroshi's memory and to explore her own talents with the pottery wheel.

She boarded a train bound for San Francisco, her suitcase filled with her favorite tools and a small collection of her most cherished pottery pieces. As the train chugged through the countryside, she gazed out the window, watching the landscape change from the familiar Southern terrain to the rolling hills and golden sunsets of the West.

Upon arriving in San Francisco, Jean Louise marveled at the city's diversity and bustling energy. She wandered the streets, taking in the sights and smells of Chinatown, the colorful houses of the Castro, and the salty air of the wharf. Her heart swelled with a sense of adventure as she booked passage on a steamer bound for Osaka, the journey ahead calling to her with the promise of new beginnings.

The voyage across the Pacific was long but invigorating. Jean Louise spent her days on the deck, watching the waves crash against the ship's hull and feeling the sun warm her face. She thought of Hiroshi and their time together, the love they had shared, and the life she hoped to build in Japan.

Upon her arrival in Osaka, Jean Louise was struck by the beauty of the city, its streets bustling with life and history. She found a small apartment in a quiet neighborhood, setting up her pottery wheel in a room that looked out over a small garden. The scent of cherry blossoms wafted through the open windows, reminding her of Hiroshi and the love they had shared.

Determined to immerse herself in the local culture, Jean Louise enrolled in a pottery class at a nearby studio. There, she found not only instruction but also friendship and support from her fellow artists. They welcomed her with open arms, sharing their knowledge and helping her to refine her craft. In return, Jean Louise shared her own experiences and the lessons she had learned from Hiroshi, creating a fusion of Southern and Japanese styles that captivated all who saw her work.

Word of her unique pottery began to spread, and soon, Jean Louise was invited to showcase her creations in galleries across Osaka. Her work was a testament to the love she and Hiroshi had shared, each piece infused with the warmth of their memories and the strength of their bond. The people of Japan embraced her art, and Jean Louise found herself becoming a bridge between two cultures, much like her children had done before her.

As the years passed, Jean Louise continued to create and share her pottery, her work becoming a symbol of love's power to transcend boundaries and bring people together. In her heart, she knew that Hiroshi would be proud of her, not only for the life she had built in Japan but also for the way she had carried on their legacy of love and acceptance.

And so, beneath the vibrant skies of Osaka, Jean Louise continued to shape clay into vessels of beauty and love, a living testament to the journey she had begun so many years ago in a small Southern diner. Her life, once bound by the prejudices of Magnolia Springs, had blossomed into a story of resilience, hope, and the transformative power of love.

Screenplay

Title: Magnolia Springs

copyright 2023 peacockOriginals.com LLC

FADE IN:

EXT. LILLY'S DINER - DAY

A small diner in the heart of Magnolia Springs. JEAN LOUISE, a young waitress, serves breakfast to the regular customers.

INT. LILLY'S DINER - DAY

HIROSHI, a Japanese salesman, enters the diner. The patrons stare at him, but he remains calm and takes a seat. Jean Louise serves him food and they strike up a conversation.

EXT. OLD OAK TREE - NIGHT

Jean Louise and Hiroshi confess their love for each other and become engaged under the old oak tree.

INT. CHURCH - DAY

Jean Louise and Hiroshi get married, despite disapproval from the townspeople.

EXT. JAPANESE VILLAGE - DAY

The couple moves to Japan, opens a pottery shop, and raises a family.

INT. POTTERY SHOP - DAY

Jean Louise and Hiroshi work together, creating beautiful pottery that reflects their love for each other.

EXT. MAGNOLIA SPRINGS - DAY

News of Jean Louise and Hiroshi's life in Japan reaches the town, slowly changing its attitudes.

EXT. GRAVESITE - DAY

Hiroshi's funeral takes place, blending Japanese and Southern traditions. Jean Louise places a small pot by his headstone.

INT. JEAN LOUISE'S HOME - DAY

Jean Louise decides to embark on a journey to San Francisco and then Osaka to explore her talents with the pottery wheel.

INT. TRAIN - DAY

Jean Louise boards the train to San Francisco, her suitcase filled with her pottery tools and cherished pieces.

EXT. SAN FRANCISCO - DAY

Jean Louise explores the city and books passage on a steamer to Osaka.

EXT. OSAKA - DAY

Jean Louise arrives in Osaka, finds an apartment, and enrolls in a pottery class, where she forms friendships and refines her craft.

INT. POTTERY STUDIO - DAY

Jean Louise creates unique pottery, combining Southern and Japanese styles. She gains recognition and showcases her work in galleries.

EXT. OSAKA - DAY

Jean Louise continues to create and share her pottery, her work becoming a symbol of love's power to transcend boundaries and bring people together.

FADE OUT.

Shooting Script

Title: Magnolia Springs

copyright 2023 peacockOriginals.com LLC

FADE IN:

EXT. LILLY'S DINER - DAY

A small diner in the heart of Magnolia Springs. JEAN LOUISE, a young waitress, serves breakfast to the regular customers.

INT. LILLY'S DINER - DAY

HIROSHI, a Japanese salesman, enters the diner. The patrons stare at him, but he remains calm and takes a seat. Jean Louise serves him food and they strike up a conversation.

Jean Louise: So, what brings you to Magnolia Springs? Hiroshi: I'm a salesman. I represent a Japanese pottery company.

EXT. OLD OAK TREE - NIGHT

Jean Louise and Hiroshi confess their love for each other and become engaged under the old oak tree.

Hiroshi: Jean Louise, will you marry me? Jean Louise: Yes, Hiroshi, with all my heart.

INT. CHURCH - DAY

Jean Louise and Hiroshi get married, despite disapproval from the townspeople.

EXT. JAPANESE VILLAGE - DAY

The couple moves to Japan, opens a pottery shop, and raises a family.

INT. POTTERY SHOP - DAY

Jean Louise and Hiroshi work together, creating beautiful pottery that reflects their love for each other.

EXT. MAGNOLIA SPRINGS - DAY

News of Jean Louise and Hiroshi's life in Japan reaches the town, slowly changing its attitudes.

EXT. GRAVESITE - DAY

Hiroshi's funeral takes place, blending Japanese and Southern traditions. Jean Louise places a small pot by his headstone.

Jean Louise: I will carry your love with me always, Hiroshi.

INT. JEAN LOUISE'S HOME - DAY

Jean Louise decides to embark on a journey to San Francisco and then Osaka to explore her talents with the pottery wheel.

INT. TRAIN - DAY

Jean Louise boards the train to San Francisco, her suitcase filled with her pottery tools and cherished pieces.

EXT. SAN FRANCISCO - DAY

Jean Louise explores the city and books passage on a steamer to Osaka.

EXT. OSAKA - DAY

Jean Louise arrives in Osaka, finds an apartment, and enrolls in a pottery class, where she forms friendships and refines her craft.

INT. POTTERY STUDIO - DAY

Jean Louise creates unique pottery, combining Southern and Japanese styles. She gains recognition and showcases her work in galleries.

EXT. OSAKA - DAY

Jean Louise continues to create and share her pottery, her work becoming a symbol of love's power to transcend boundaries and bring people together.

FADE OUT.

Fortune's Wheel

[in the style of William Shakespeare]

In fair London, where we lay our scene,

From ancient grime to new prosperity,

A tale unfolds, of youth and sweet ambition,

Where orphans strive and stars align in constellations.

In days of yore, a ship from farthest Ind

Discharged its cargo and its crew upon

The teeming wharves of London's murky Thames.

Among the swarthy sailors disembarked,

A boy, an orphan of a tender age,

His eyes alight with dreams of fortune's gifts.

This callow youth, our hero christened Jack,

Had neither sire nor dam to call his own,

His fate consigned to ocean's vast embrace.

But London's sirens, with their dulcet tones,

Did lull him from the ship that bore him hence,

And so our Jack did jump o'erboard one night,

To seek his fortune in the city's arms.

He wandered far, this waif of foreign shores,

And soon did find himself in Shoreditch fair,

Where playwrights, poets, actors did convene,

To tell their tales and share their artful trade.

A troupe of players, clad in motley garb,

Did capture Jack's young heart with passion's fire.

And so, with eager heart and nimble step,

He sought to join the motley company,

To learn the art of mimicry and speech,

And rise, perchance, to be a star of note.

But first, a humble page he was to be,

To sweep the stage, and tend to every want

Of haughty actors, full of pride and bile.

In time, as Fortune's wheel doth turn for all,

Young Jack did earn the notice of the great,

A playwright famed for wit and learned quill,

Who took the orphaned boy beneath his wing,

And taught him all the secrets of the stage,

To speak the verse, to cry, to laugh, to rage.

As years did pass, and Jack did grow in skill,

His star ascended o'er the London stage,

And audiences did thrill to see him act,

In tragedies, comedies, histories too,

This orphan boy, once found amongst the rats,

Did now command the hearts of high and low.

One fateful eve, in royal presence staged,

Our Jack performed a scene of love and loss,

And as he spoke, the very air did still,

His voice a river, soft and bittersweet,

Enraptured all, from pauper to the king.

His fame thus sealed, his fortune now assured,

Our Jack, once orphaned, ship-jumped, and unknown,

Did take his place amongst the stars of old,

His name inscribed upon the rolls of fame.

His tale, a testament to those who strive,

In Fortune's fickle path, to find their way,

And prove that dreams can rise from humble birth,

To light the stage, and burnish history's page.

And so, our Jack, a phoenix born anew,

From humble origins did rise and soar,

And yet, a longing still did gnaw his heart,

For fame and fortune could not fill the void,

That absence of a family did leave.

One day, as Jack walked London's bustling streets,

He chanced upon a tavern warm and bright,

And in its glow, he spied a band of men,

Their laughter loud, their camaraderie clear.

These sailors, fresh from voyage on the sea,

Did stir within our Jack a distant pang,

A memory of days upon the waves,

When he, a boy, did leap from ship to shore.

He joined the men and shared a hearty ale,

And as they spoke, a tale began to form,

A play, a drama born from sea and salt,

A story of an orphan finding home,

Amidst the swell and storm of life's tempests.

This inspiration struck our Jack like lightning,

He seized the quill and penned the tale with haste.

The play, when finished, was presented true,

Upon the stage where Jack had found his fame,

And as the final curtain closed upon

The heartfelt tale of wanderers and kin,

The audience rose, with tears upon their cheeks,

To laud the work of one who'd found his way,

From ship to stage, from orphan to the Bard.

Our Jack, now known as playwright and as actor,

Did find within his heart a peace and warmth,

For though he'd never known a family's love,

He'd forged a bond with those who shared his art,

A brotherhood of players, proud and true,

Who trod the boards and brought his tales to life.

And so, our tale draws to a close, my friends,
The story of an orphan boy who dared,
To dream, to strive, to climb from low to high,
And find his place amongst the stars above.
Let us remember Jack, and all like him,
Who brave the world with naught but hope and heart,
And know that e'en the humblest of beginnings,
Can birth a legend, ne'er to be forgot.

Screenplay

Title: Fortune's Wheel

copyright 2023 peacockOriginals.com LLC

Act I:

Scene 1: A bustling London dock

1. (Sailors unload cargo from a large ship while young Jack watches)
2. (Jack jumps from the ship and swims ashore, unnoticed by the sailors)
3. (He wanders the streets of London, observing the various trades and businesses)

Scene 2: Shoreditch, a troupe of players performing on the street

1. (Jack happens upon the players and is captivated by their performance)
2. (After the performance, Jack approaches the players and asks to join their troupe)
3. (The players agree to take Jack on as a page, sweeping the stage and attending to their needs)

Act II:

Scene 1: The theater, Jack's first day

1. (Jack learns the ropes from the playwright and the actors, working diligently)
2. (Over time, Jack's talent for acting is noticed by the playwright)
3. (The playwright takes Jack under his wing, teaching him the art of acting)

Scene 2: Jack's rise to fame

1. (Jack performs in various plays, earning a reputation as a talented actor)

2. (The King attends one of Jack's performances, and Jack's fame is cemented)
3. (Despite his success, Jack feels an emptiness inside)

Act III:

Scene 1: A tavern filled with sailors
1. (Jack encounters sailors and joins them for drinks and stories)
2. (Inspired by their camaraderie, Jack begins to write a play about his own journey)
3. (Jack completes the play, a story of an orphan finding home amidst the storms of life)

Scene 2: The premiere of Jack's play
1. (The play is performed to great acclaim, with Jack starring in the lead role)
2. (The audience is moved to tears, and Jack's status as a playwright is solidified)
3. (Jack finds peace and warmth in his newfound family of fellow actors and playwrights)

Epilogue:
1. (Jack, now known as the Bard, continues to write and perform plays)
2. (He remains a legend in the world of theater, his journey inspiring generations to come)
3. (The curtain falls, signaling the end of Jack's tale and his rise from ship to stage)

Shooting Script

Title: Fortune's Wheel

copyright 2023 peacockOriginals.com LLC

INT. LONDON DOCK - DAY

A bustling dock, SAILORS unload cargo from a large ship, shouting and laughing. YOUNG JACK (13) watches from the ship's deck, eyes wide with curiosity.

EXT. LONDON DOCK - DAY

Jack, taking a deep breath, jumps from the ship and swims ashore, unnoticed by the sailors. He pulls himself onto the dock, soaked and shivering.

EXT. LONDON STREETS - DAY

Jack wanders the streets of London, observing the various trades and businesses, lost in the unfamiliar world.

EXT. SHOREDITCH - DAY

Jack happens upon a TROUPE OF PLAYERS performing on the street, captivating the audience. Jack is mesmerized by their performance.

EXT. SHOREDITCH - DAY - LATER

After the performance, Jack approaches the LEAD ACTOR and the PLAYWRIGHT, asking to join their troupe. They exchange glances before agreeing to take Jack on as a page.

INT. THEATER - DAY

Jack sweeps the stage, attending to the needs of the haughty actors. He watches them rehearse with longing.

INT. THEATER - NIGHT

The playwright takes Jack aside, teaching him the art of acting. Jack absorbs the lessons, practicing with fervor.

INT. THEATER - NIGHT - MONTHS LATER

Jack performs in various plays, earning a reputation as a talented actor. The theater fills with adoring fans.

INT. THEATER - NIGHT - ROYAL PERFORMANCE

The KING attends one of Jack's performances. Jack, now an adult (25), delivers a breathtaking monologue. The audience, including the King, applauds thunderously.

INT. TAVERN - NIGHT

Jack, feeling the emptiness of success, encounters SAILORS at a tavern. He joins them for drinks and stories, laughing heartily.

INT. JACK'S ROOM - NIGHT

Inspired by the sailors' camaraderie, Jack writes a play about his own journey late into the night.

INT. THEATER - NIGHT - PLAY PREMIERE

Jack's play premieres to great acclaim, with Jack starring in the lead role. The audience is moved to tears.

INT. THEATER - NIGHT - AFTER THE PERFORMANCE

Jack, surrounded by his fellow actors, playwrights, and friends, finds peace and warmth in his newfound family.

EXT. THEATER - NIGHT - EPILOGUE

The theater marquee displays Jack's name as the Bard. The legend of Jack's journey continues to inspire generations.

FADE OUT.

Finn in Mongoose Land

[in the style of C.S. Lewis]

Once upon a time, in a small coastal village nestled between the majestic mountains and the vast ocean, there lived a young boy named Finn. Finn was a curious and adventurous soul, with a sun-kissed complexion and an unruly mop of curly hair that spoke of his love for the sea. From the moment he could stand, he had been drawn to the water, a natural-born surfer boy.

As the sun rose each morning, Finn would pick up his trusty surfboard, a gift from his father, and head down to the shore. The villagers often whispered amongst themselves that the sea and the boy had a special bond, like two old friends who could communicate without words.

One day, as Finn was exploring the nearby rocky cliffs after a particularly thrilling surf session, he stumbled upon a small cave. The cave was barely visible, hidden behind an overgrowth of wild vines and moss. A faint shimmer of blue light emitted from within, piquing Finn's curiosity.

As he cautiously stepped inside, he discovered a small creature nestled among the moss and pebbles. It was a mongoose, but unlike any he had ever seen before. Its fur seemed to shimmer with an otherworldly glow, and its eyes were a deep, enchanting shade of violet. The mongoose looked up at Finn, and to his astonishment, it spoke.

"Hello, young surfer," it said, its voice a curious blend of soft whispers and musical notes. "I have been waiting for you."

Finn blinked in disbelief, certain that he must be dreaming. "You can talk?"

"I am no ordinary mongoose," the creature replied. "I have been blessed with certain magical powers. My name is Lyra, and I have been waiting for someone with a heart as pure and adventurous as yours."

Finn hesitated, still unsure whether to believe the strange, talking mongoose. "Why me? What do you want from me?"

"I need your help, Finn," Lyra said earnestly. "There is a great darkness threatening our world, and I have been tasked with finding the one who can help restore the balance. I believe that person is you."

Over the next few days, Finn and Lyra became inseparable, as the mongoose taught Finn about her magical abilities. She could shape-shift, heal wounds, and even manipulate the elements. Finn discovered that he, too, had untapped potential – the bond he shared with the sea was far more powerful than he had ever realized.

As they trained together, they learned to harness their combined powers, using the ocean as their ally. Finn's surfboard became a conduit for their magic, growing stronger and more responsive with each passing day.

The day of reckoning finally came when a monstrous wave, unlike any seen before, rose from the depths of the ocean. It threatened to engulf the entire village, driven by the very darkness that Lyra had warned Finn about.

As the villagers panicked, Finn and Lyra stood together on the shore, their hearts heavy with the weight of their responsibility. With the villagers' lives at stake, they knew that they had to confront the darkness head-on.

Lyra climbed onto Finn's surfboard, and together, they charged toward the monstrous wave. The boy and the mongoose, united by the power of friendship and the magic they had learned to wield, called upon the ocean to join their fight.

With a mighty roar, the water surged around them, transforming into a dazzling display of light and energy. Finn and Lyra rode the crest of the wave, their eyes locked onto the heart of the darkness.

As they reached the peak, the darkness seemed to falter, sensing their unwavering determination. Finn and Lyra poured every ounce of their power into one final, resounding battle cry, and with that, the darkness shattered like glass, its fragments dissipating into the air.

The wave that had threatened to destroy the village now receded, gently washing over the shore as if to apologize for its earlier fury. The villagers, who had watched the entire spectacle unfold, erupted into cheers and applause. They embraced Finn and Lyra as heroes, grateful for their bravery and sacrifice.

As the sun began to set, casting its warm, golden light across the village, Finn and Lyra knew that their work was done. The darkness had been vanquished, and the balance of their world restored.

In the days that followed, Finn and Lyra continued to explore the ocean together, their bond growing stronger with each passing moment. The village, too, learned to respect and appreciate the magic that lived within their midst, no longer fearing the power of the sea.

And so, the story of the surfer boy and the magical mongoose became a beloved legend in the small coastal village, a tale passed down through generations as a reminder of the power of friendship, courage, and the magic that lies hidden in the hearts of those who dare to believe.

Screenplay

Title: Finn in Mongoose Land

copyright 2023 peacockOriginals.com LLC

INT. FINN'S HOME - MORNING

Finn, a young surfer boy with sun-kissed skin and unruly curly hair, picks up his surfboard, a gift from his father, and heads out the door.

EXT. VILLAGE SHORE - MORNING

Finn skillfully rides the waves as the villagers watch in awe, whispering about his special bond with the sea.

EXT. ROCKY CLIFFS - DAY

Finn explores the cliffs and discovers a hidden cave, emitting a faint blue light.

INT. HIDDEN CAVE - DAY

Finn cautiously steps inside the cave and finds Lyra, a mongoose with shimmering fur and deep violet eyes. Lyra speaks to Finn.

LYRA Hello, young surfer. I have been waiting for you.

FINN (looking astonished) You can talk?

LYRA I am no ordinary mongoose. I have been blessed with magical powers. My name is Lyra, and I have been waiting for someone with a heart as pure and adventurous as yours.

EXT. VILLAGE SHORE - DAY

Finn and Lyra spend their days training together, discovering their combined powers and learning to harness the ocean's energy.

EXT. VILLAGE SHORE - DAY

A monstrous wave rises from the depths of the ocean, threatening to engulf the village. Panic ensues.

Finn and Lyra stand together on the shore, prepared to face the darkness.

EXT. VILLAGE SHORE - MOMENTS LATER

Finn and Lyra ride toward the monstrous wave on Finn's surfboard, calling upon the ocean's power to aid them in their fight.

As they reach the peak of the wave, Finn and Lyra unleash their combined magic, shattering the darkness and restoring balance to their world.

EXT. VILLAGE SHORE - DAY

The villagers celebrate Finn and Lyra as heroes, embracing them with gratitude.

EXT. VILLAGE SHORE - SUNSET

Finn and Lyra continue to explore the ocean together, their bond growing stronger.

FADE OUT.

Shooting Script

Title: Finn in Mongoose Land

copyright 2023 peacockOriginals.com LLC

EXT. VILLAGE SHORE - MORNING

A picturesque coastal village sits nestled between mountains and the ocean. Finn, a young surfer boy with sun-kissed skin and unruly curly hair, picks up his surfboard and heads out the door.

EXT. VILLAGE SHORE - CONTINUOUS

Finn skillfully rides the waves. The villagers watch in awe, whispering among themselves.

EXT. ROCKY CLIFFS - DAY

Finn explores the cliffs, discovering a hidden cave emitting a faint blue light.

INT. HIDDEN CAVE - CONTINUOUS

Finn cautiously steps inside, finding Lyra, a mongoose with shimmering fur and deep violet eyes. Lyra speaks.

LYRA Hello, young surfer. I have been waiting for you.

FINN (astonished) You can talk?

LYRA I am no ordinary mongoose. I have magical powers. My name is Lyra, and I have been waiting for someone with a heart as pure and adventurous as yours.

EXT. VILLAGE SHORE - DAY - MONTAGE

Finn and Lyra spend their days together:

- Lyra shape-shifts, revealing her various abilities

- Finn discovers his connection to the sea is stronger than he thought
- The pair train, learning to harness their powers

EXT. VILLAGE SHORE - DAY

A monstrous wave rises from the ocean, threatening the village. Panic ensues. Finn and Lyra stand together on the shore, prepared to face the darkness.

EXT. VILLAGE SHORE - MOMENTS LATER

Finn and Lyra ride toward the monstrous wave on Finn's surfboard. They call upon the ocean's power to aid them in their fight.

EXT. VILLAGE SHORE - CONTINUOUS

Finn and Lyra reach the peak of the wave. They unleash their combined magic, shattering the darkness and restoring balance to their world.

EXT. VILLAGE SHORE - DAY

The villagers celebrate Finn and Lyra as heroes, embracing them with gratitude.

EXT. VILLAGE SHORE - SUNSET

Finn and Lyra continue to explore the ocean together, their bond growing stronger.

FADE OUT.

One, Two, Many

[in the style of Danielle Steel]

Amber Dubois, a young woman from New York City, had been eagerly anticipating her ten-day vacation to Jamaica. As a hardworking college student, she was in dire need of an escape from the hustle and bustle of the city. The trip was a graduation gift from her doting parents and she was going with her closest college friends.

They had all been planning this adventure for months, envisioning themselves on white sandy beaches, sipping cocktails while the Caribbean sun kissed their skin.

Upon arriving in Montego Bay, Amber and her friends were greeted by a cacophony of vibrant colors and the warm, balmy air. They quickly settled into their luxurious resort, eager to soak up the exotic atmosphere. That evening, they decided to unwind at the resort's beachside bar, where they could indulge in the island's famous rum cocktails.

Amber, dressed in a flowy white sundress, was captivated by the bar's ambiance. The sound of reggae music filled the air, blending harmoniously with the distant crash of waves on the shore. Her green eyes sparkled with excitement as she scanned the room, and then she saw him.

He was tall, dark, and disarmingly handsome. As if reading her thoughts, the Jamaican bartender caught her gaze and flashed a dazzling smile. He approached the group, introducing himself as Julian. His deep voice, tinged with a musical Jamaican accent, sent shivers down Amber's spine. From that moment, she knew she was irrevocably drawn to him.

Over the next few days, Amber and Julian's connection deepened. They spent hours talking and laughing, their chemistry undeniable. The more time they spent together, the more infatuated Amber became. She was enthralled by his charm, his passion for life, and his captivating stories about the island's folklore and traditions.

One evening, Julian invited Amber on a moonlit stroll along the beach. As they walked hand in hand, the moon cast a silver glow on the water, and the sea breeze whispered through the palm trees. It felt like a scene from a romance novel, and Amber's heart swelled with a mixture of happiness and fear. She knew she was falling dangerously in love with Julian.

As their vacation neared its end, Amber's friends began to notice the change in her. They worried about her obsession with Julian, sensing that it was beginning to consume her. They gently tried to remind her that once they returned to New York City, the fairy tale would end, and reality would set in.

But Amber was in too deep. The last night of their trip, she made a rash decision to stay in Jamaica, convinced that her future was with Julian. Her friends tearfully said their goodbyes, hoping Amber would come to her senses soon.

Despite her friends' warnings, Amber was blind to the darkness that lurked beneath Julian's alluring exterior. It was only after she stayed that she discovered the truth. Julian was entangled in a dangerous underworld, filled with crime and deception. His charm and good looks were merely a facade, designed to lure unsuspecting victims into his twisted world.

Amber found herself trapped, her life now in constant peril. Her once enchanting love affair had turned into a nightmare, leaving her desperate for a way out. She realized that her infatuation had blinded her to the danger she now faced.

In a daring attempt to escape, Amber managed to contact her friends back home. With their help, she was able to flee Jamaica and return to the safety of New York City. The experience left her shaken, but wiser. She vowed to never again let infatuation cloud her judgment, and to always cherish the friends who had saved her from the deadly grasp of her intoxicating Jamaican bartender.

As Amber settled back into her life in New York City, she carried the painful lessons of her Jamaican misadventure with her. She focused on rebuilding her life, finishing her studies, and finding a career. However, the memories of her time in Jamaica never left her, serving as a constant reminder of the perils of blind infatuation.

Her friends, who had been there for her when she needed them the most, remained a constant support system. They had been her lifeline when she was lost in the darkness, and Amber found comfort in their unwavering friendship.

Years passed, and Amber's life took on a rhythm of its own. She found success in her career and even managed to find love again, this time with a kind, dependable man named Michael. He was the antithesis of Julian, his love a gentle balm that soothed the scars left by her past.

One day, Amber stumbled upon an old photograph from her fateful trip to Jamaica. As she studied the picture of her younger self, surrounded by her friends and glowing with happiness, she felt a bittersweet pang in her heart. While that chapter of her life had been marked by pain and deception, it had also taught her invaluable lessons.

She was grateful for the experiences that had shaped her, for they had molded her into the strong, resilient woman she had become. Amber had learned the hard way that love should never be blind, and that true friendship was the most precious treasure of all. With these lessons etched in her heart, she moved forward in her life, embracing the wisdom and strength born from the shadows of her past.

Amber's life in New York City continued to flourish. She and Michael had recently moved into a cozy brownstone in Brooklyn, and their love had grown stronger with each passing day. Her friends remained by her side, steadfast and supportive as ever.

One day, as Amber left her office in Manhattan, she felt a sudden chill down her spine, as if she was being watched. She quickly scanned the busy street, but saw nothing out of the ordinary. Shaking off the feeling, she continued on her way, unaware that her past was about to catch up with her.

Several days later, Amber found herself in a trendy coffee shop, enjoying an afternoon latte with her friend, Sarah. They were deep in conversation, reminiscing about their college days and laughing over shared memories, when Sarah's eyes widened in shock.

"Amber," Sarah whispered, her voice trembling. "Don't look now, but I think Julian is here."

Amber's heart began to race as she cautiously turned her head to see him. There, at the other end of the coffee shop, stood Julian, his dark eyes locked on her. It had been years since she had last seen him, and yet, his handsome face still had the power to stir something within her.

As Amber's mind raced, a thousand questions flooded her thoughts. How had Julian found her? What did he want? Was she in danger? She knew she couldn't let him back into her life, but a small part of her still longed for the magnetic connection they had once shared.

Noticing her hesitation, Sarah grabbed Amber's hand and whispered, "We need to leave, now."

Together, they slipped out of the coffee shop, hearts pounding in their chests. Amber couldn't shake the feeling that she was being hunted, and she knew she had to confront Julian before he could threaten her newfound happiness.

With the support of Michael and her friends, Amber devised a plan to confront Julian and protect herself from any potential harm. They enlisted the help of a private investigator, who uncovered the truth about Julian's activities since their time in Jamaica. He had continued his life of crime, leaving a trail of heartbreak and destruction in his wake.

The knowledge that she had narrowly escaped a life of torment and despair fortified Amber's resolve. She was no longer the naive girl who had fallen for Julian's charms; she was a woman who had fought her way back from the brink of darkness and had everything to lose.

When the time came for Amber to face Julian, she was surrounded by her loved ones, their presence a reminder of her strength and determination. As she stared into the eyes of the man who had once ensnared her heart, Amber spoke with a newfound authority.

"Julian, your presence here threatens everything I've worked so hard to rebuild. You need to leave, and never come back," she declared, her voice unwavering.

To her surprise, Julian didn't put up a fight. He seemed almost haunted, as if the weight of his own demons had finally caught up with him. He nodded solemnly and walked away, disappearing into the bustling streets of New York City.

With Julian gone, Amber was finally free to embrace her future without fear. She had faced her past head-on, and it no longer held any power over her. As she continued her journey, hand in hand with Michael and her friends, she knew that she had emerged victorious from the darkest chapter of her life, her love and friendships more precious than ever.

Screenplay

Title: One, Two, Many

copyright 2023 peacockOriginals.com LLC

INT. AMBER'S APARTMENT - DAY

Amber and her friends, SARAH, LUCY, and EMMA, are excitedly packing for their ten-day vacation to Jamaica.

SARAH (while folding a swimsuit) I can't believe we're finally going! I need this vacation so badly.

LUCY Same here. This semester was brutal.

EMMA (giggles) We're going to have the best time!

EXT. MONTEGO BAY RESORT - DAY

Amber and her friends arrive at the luxurious resort, taking in the vibrant colors and atmosphere of Jamaica.

INT. BEACHSIDE BAR - NIGHT

The group enjoys their first night in Jamaica. Amber, wearing a flowy white sundress, scans the room and catches sight of JULIAN, the handsome bartender.

JULIAN (approaching the group) Welcome! I'm Julian. What can I get you ladies to drink?

The girls place their orders, and Amber can't help but feel drawn to Julian.

EXT. BEACH - NIGHT (MONTAGE)

Amber and Julian's relationship develops, as they spend time laughing, talking, and walking on the beach.

INT. AMBER'S HOTEL ROOM - DAY

Amber's friends express their concerns about her growing obsession with Julian.

LUCY Amber, we're worried about you. This thing with Julian... It's consuming you.

EMMA We're leaving in two days. You need to think about what happens when we go back to New York.

Amber dismisses their concerns, and the conversation ends tensely.

EXT. BEACH - NIGHT

Amber tells Julian her decision to stay in Jamaica. They embrace, but the moment is bittersweet.

INT. NEW YORK CITY APARTMENT - NIGHT

Amber, now back in New York, is on a video call with Sarah, Lucy, and Emma, who express relief at her safe return.

EXT. BROOKLYN BROWNSTONE - DAY

Amber and her boyfriend, MICHAEL, move into their new home together.

INT. COFFEE SHOP - DAY

Amber and Sarah sit together, deep in conversation, when Sarah notices Julian at the other end of the shop.

SARAH (whispering) Amber, don't look now, but I think Julian is here.

Amber turns and sees Julian, his eyes locked on her. They hastily leave the coffee shop.

INT. AMBER'S BROWNSTONE - NIGHT

Amber, Michael, Sarah, Lucy, and Emma discuss how to confront Julian and protect Amber from potential danger.

EXT. CENTRAL PARK - DAY

Amber, accompanied by her friends, confronts Julian. She speaks with newfound authority and demands that he leave her life forever. Julian walks away without a fight.

EXT. NEW YORK CITY STREET - DAY

Amber, Michael, and her friends walk together, victorious and ready to embrace the future.

FADE OUT.

THE END

Shooting Script

Title: One, Two, Many

copyright 2023 peacockOriginals.com LLC

INT. AMBER'S APARTMENT - DAY

CLOSE UP on a SUITCASE as Amber and her friends, SARAH, LUCY, and EMMA, excitedly pack for their ten-day vacation to Jamaica.

SARAH (while folding a swimsuit) I can't believe we're finally going! I need this vacation so badly.

LUCY Same here. This semester was brutal.

EMMA (giggles) We're going to have the best time!

EXT. MONTEGO BAY RESORT - DAY - ESTABLISHING SHOT

Amber and her friends arrive at the luxurious resort, taking in the vibrant colors and atmosphere of Jamaica.

INT. BEACHSIDE BAR - NIGHT

WIDE SHOT of the group enjoying their first night in Jamaica. PAN to Amber, wearing a flowy white sundress, as she scans the room and catches sight of JULIAN, the handsome bartender.

JULIAN (approaching the group) Welcome! I'm Julian. What can I get you ladies to drink?

The girls place their orders, and Amber can't help but feel drawn to Julian.

EXT. BEACH - NIGHT (MONTAGE)

Various shots of Amber and Julian's relationship developing, as they spend time laughing, talking, and walking on the beach.

INT. AMBER'S HOTEL ROOM - DAY

Amber's friends express their concerns about her growing obsession with Julian.

LUCY Amber, we're worried about you. This thing with Julian... It's consuming you.

EMMA We're leaving in two days. You need to think about what happens when we go back to New York.

Amber dismisses their concerns, and the conversation ends tensely.

EXT. BEACH - NIGHT

Amber tells Julian her decision to stay in Jamaica. They embrace, but the moment is bittersweet.

INT. NEW YORK CITY APARTMENT - NIGHT

Amber, now back in New York, is on a video call with Sarah, Lucy, and Emma, who express relief at her safe return.

EXT. BROOKLYN BROWNSTONE - DAY

Amber and her boyfriend, MICHAEL, move into their new home together.

INT. COFFEE SHOP - DAY

Amber and Sarah sit together, deep in conversation, when Sarah notices Julian at the other end of the shop.

SARAH (whispering) Amber, don't look now, but I think Julian is here.

Amber turns and sees Julian, his eyes locked on her. They hastily leave the coffee shop.

INT. AMBER'S BROWNSTONE - NIGHT

Amber, Michael, Sarah, Lucy, and Emma discuss how to confront Julian and protect Amber from potential danger.

EXT. CENTRAL PARK - DAY

Amber, accompanied by her friends, confronts Julian. She speaks with newfound authority and demands that he leave her life forever. Julian walks away without a fight.

EXT. NEW YORK CITY STREET - DAY

Amber, Michael, and her friends walk together, victorious and ready to embrace the future.

FADE OUT.

THE END

Colophon 3.0

[in the style of Everett Peacock]

audio that helped guide the creative process

the rare silence in Lahaina found only for a moment or two in the early hours; the dripping coffee juice slowly filling the self heating mug my Mom got me for a birthday; crowing roosters unsure why they feel so compelled to yell all the time; the nearly silent arrival of a large cruise ship before dawn, its diesel engines painting the still waters between there and the beach with a distinctive hum; the bedroom fan bravely trying to battle the tropical heat; the afternoon banter of YouTube tutorials on AI; the sad commentaries on how AI will kill us all – at least until I can change the "channel"; the daydreams that tease me with the amplification of creativity, and efficiency that all these new tools are promising, and delivering.

~ ALOHA ~

more free-range, organic stories & films at

peacockOriginals.com

Made in the USA
Columbia, SC
22 May 2023